The Lace Dowry

The Lace Dowry

ANDREA CHENG

*to Bee Cullinan—
with thanks—
Andrea Cheng*

FRONT STREET
Asheville, North Carolina

Library of Congress Cataloging-in-Publication Data

Cheng, Andrea.
The lace dowry / Andrea Cheng.—1st ed.
p. cm.
Summary: In Hungary in 1933, a twelve-year-old from Budapest
befriends the Halas village family of lacemakers hired to stitch her dowry.
ISBN 1-932425-20-9 (alk. paper)
[1. Friendship—Fiction. 2. Sex role—Fiction.
3. Lace makers—Fiction.
4. Hungary—History—1918-1945—Fiction.] I. Title.
PZ7.C41943Lac 2005
[Fic]—dc22
2004021186

FRONT STREET
A Division of Boyds Mills Press, Inc.
A Highlights Company

To Kati and the memory of Oma

The Lace Dowry

Chapter One

"Today we will take the train to Halas," Mama says.

I am drinking cocoa and reading my new book about Admiral Byrd's voyage to Antarctica.

"Juli, how many times do I have to tell you that we don't read at the table?" Mama's voice is too loud for the morning. "Today we are going to Halas."

I put my finger on the last word I read, *iceberg*, and look up. "I'm staying home."

"No, Juli, you are coming. We have very important business there." Mama pulls her eyebrows together.

I can see the map of Hungary in my mind. We have to copy it over and over in geography class, labeling all the major rivers and cities. I know Kiskunhalas, or Halas as Mama says, is somewhere south of Budapest. But what could possibly be so important there?

"Halas is not just any small town, Juli," Mama says. She turns to my father for help, but he is reading the newspaper. "Why is it that this family is always reading?"

Papa looks up. "Halas, did you say? Yes, of course. Halas is famous for its lace."

Now I remember that the geography teacher said something about Halas lace, but I was too busy reading *Oliver Twist* to really listen. I go back to my book. Some of the sled dogs are no longer able to walk. Their paws are frozen.

Mama shuts my book. "Juli, when we are eating breakfast, you will not read."

"But Papa rea—"

Mama cuts me off. "Hurry and get ready. We are leaving in twenty minutes." She pulls at my nightgown. "Wear the red skirt, the velvet one from your aunt Agnes."

"I don't want to go," I say, trying to find my page.

"Juli, listen to me. We will go to Halas and have the ladies make us the most beautiful lace you have ever seen. It must be big, big as this table." Mama puts her arms out to show me the size.

"We already have so many tablecloths," I say. Mama has a whole shelf in the linen closet with nothing but embroidered napkins, centerpieces, and tablecloths.

"But they are not made out of lace," Mama says. "And this one is not for me."

"Who is it for?"

Mama smiles. "For you."

"What do I want with a tablecloth?"

Mama strokes my curly hair. "This will be part of your dowry," she says.

Dowry. The word sounds like something from the Middle

Ages. "Mama, it is 1933 and I don't need a dowry," I say quickly. "Nobody in Budapest has a dowry anymore."

"But you are not nobody," Mama says.

Papa stands next to Mama in his underclothes as she irons his shirt. I know he doesn't want to go to Halas either. He wants to play chess with his old friend Lajos Bacsi. That's what he does every weekend and even some evenings on his way home from the office. After eight hours of entering numbers into a ledger book, he needs something to clear his head. Sometimes on the weekend I go with him and play with the chess pieces he has captured. Maybe Lajos Bacsi's niece Sari will be there. She and her mother live in a small town on the Danube, and sometimes they spend their weekends in Budapest. I love to hear the way Sari talks, with the *r*'s rolled deep in her throat. She always says to me, "Juli, when I get big, I'll live in Budapest like you." We play hide-and-seek behind the chairs, and when we're tired, Papa buys each of us an ice cream cone.

"How about we wait a bit," Papa says. "Look at our Juli. A girl of only twelve. I'm not sure we have to worry about a dowry just yet."

"Or ever," I mumble.

"The lace may take years to complete," Mama says. "Twelve now and eighteen before you know it. We must get started." She unplugs the iron and holds up the crisp white shirt. "What, do you want our Juli to marry a poor peasant and work herself to the bone? Now get ready."

Papa looks as if he knows it is useless to argue, but still

he has not given up. "Why go to Halas for lace when I can simply ask Lajos Bacsi to set aside a gold necklace? He's the best jeweler in all of Budapest, you know. Whatever we want, he will make."

"An ordinary necklace for our Juli? What, so you want her to find an ordinary husband? How can jewelry compare with lace from Halas?" Mama hands Papa his good black trousers. "We're leaving in five minutes," she says.

Chapter Two

The window of the train is dirty and everything is wet and gray—the fields, the barns, the small stucco houses with thatched roofs.

"I bet Sari is waiting for me," I whisper to Papa.

"And Lajos Bacsi is waiting for me," he says.

Mama hears us. "Let them wait," she says. "But we will be ready."

"Ready for what?"

"Your wedding day."

"I'm never getting married."

"Juli, don't talk nonsense."

"Mama, how can you—"

Mama puts her hand on my leg. "Shhh, Juli, no need to advertise our business to the whole world."

Why is Mama talking about the whole world? The only other person in the train compartment is a sleeping lady. I look out the window again. Two small boys are walking along a muddy road. I wonder where they are going in this rain.

I open my book and try to read, but the swaying of the train makes my stomach churn. Papa takes out a loaf of bread. He cuts a piece of salami, peels it, puts it on the bread, and offers it to me, but I shake my head. I put my head against the glass and doze.

How can Mama even think about a dowry? But I know what Papa will say if I complain. *Try to understand. Your mother was born and raised in the countryside. Her ways might be different, but she only wants what's best for you.*

The train lurches to a stop at a small station. *Kunszentmiklos* is written on the sign. Two men get on. They are missing most of their teeth, although they are younger than Papa. Mama turns away. I know she is hoping that they won't choose to sit near us. These are ordinary people, country people. They don't take care of their teeth. They wear baggy pants worn thin at the knees. We are not like them. The men pass us and go into the next car. Mama pats my arm and offers me a piece of candy.

I shake my head.

"Eat something, Juli."

"I'm not hungry."

The train is on its way again. Soon Papa is asleep. His glasses are slipping down his nose. Mama takes them off gently, folds them, and puts them into her purse. I lean against the cool glass of the train window again and try to sleep.

"We're here."

Mama pokes Papa with her elbow. He stands up groggily.

"Tuck in your shirt, Juli," she says. "And stand up straight."

My posture is one of Mama's biggest problems. I slouch, she says, to hide my height.

We stand on the platform underneath the *Halas* sign. It's still raining, but the sky is starting to lighten up. "How do we know which way to go?" I ask.

Mama waves a slip of paper. "Aunt Zsofi gave me the name of the best lace maker in town. All the ladies in Halas make lace, and from what I hear, they often work together, but this one is…" Mama kisses her fingertips to show us how special the lady is.

Mama hands us each an umbrella from her bag and we head away from the station on a small dirt road. Mama takes my arm. "The Halas lace is the most famous in the world, Juli. Even more famous than the Belgian lace that we hear so much about."

I don't know what Mama is talking about. I never even heard of Belgian lace.

"Lace is lace," I say.

"No, Juli. Lace is not lace. Just ask Papa. That's like telling Lajos Bacsi that one diamond is like the next. But that is not so, is it, Papa?"

"You're right," Papa says.

Mama goes on. "That's like saying one man is as good as the next. No, Juli, that's not the way the world works." Mama pulls me around a big puddle. "A small piece of Halas lace was presented to the princess of Holland to celebrate her coronation."

I want to tell Mama that I am not a princess, so I have no

need for a lace anything, but she is pulling me along so fast that my shoulder hurts. Mud is splashing on my new stockings. I cannot imagine fine white lace in this muddy village. A chicken is standing in the middle of the road. Suddenly it ruffles its feathers and runs at my legs. I scream and run to hide behind Papa.

"Scared of a chicken, are you?" Papa kicks at the bird until it flutters to the side of the road.

"Juli, please watch where you are going." Mama tries to brush the mud off my stockings, but it only smears. She stops for a minute and squints into the drizzle. "I think it's that farm right there." She points to a small house in the distance with a barn next to it. "Aunt Zsofi said it was up a small hill."

"Are they expecting us?" Papa asks.

"Expecting? Of course. Aunt Zsofi told them weeks ago that we would be coming to place an order."

My legs are tired, and the umbrella is making my arm sore. "It stopped raining," I say, stopping to close my umbrella.

Mama puts her umbrella down and looks up at the sky to see if I am telling the truth. "Well, it might just start again," she says, putting it back up and pulling me along.

When finally we get close to the house, Papa takes a deep breath. "And how much are we to offer for this lace?" he asks.

"Leave it to me," Mama says.

"Then why am I here?" Papa mumbles under his breath.

"What was that?"

Papa's eyes meet mine. "Nothing."

Chapter Three

When we get to the door of the house, two small boys and a bigger girl stare at us. The boys run to hide behind their mother's chair. The girl is watching me. "Somebody's here," she says without turning around.

"Tell your mother that the Kis family is here from Budapest," Mama says. There is only one room in the house, so the girl's mother can hear everything we say. "We have come to place an order."

The lady doesn't say anything.

"We have come to order lace for my daughter's dowry," Mama says. She pushes me from behind. "You can see she is already big."

The lady moves her eyes quickly from my head to my feet. I feel the blood rush to my face, and I hunch my shoulders.

Mama pokes the middle of my back. "Stand up straight," she whispers to me. Then, louder, she says to the lady, "A tablecloth is what we have in mind."

"Not a tablecloth," the lady says abruptly. "A centerpiece."

"What I'd like," Mama says, "is a tablecloth like this." Mama makes a big circle with her arms.

The lady shakes her head. "Too big. Like this." She makes a small frame with her fingers.

"Mrs. Voros," Mama says, "you must understand. We have only one daughter. We need only one dowry. And this dowry is to be the biggest, most beautiful lace in the world."

"This big," the lady says again, making her frame slightly larger.

Mama knits her brow. Papa tries to whisper something to her, but she waves him away. "Let's make an arrangement. We will come every other month. Each time we come, you show us two squares like this." Mama makes a frame with her hands. "And when you have enough squares, you put them together into one big tablecloth."

The lady sighs. "And when you come, what will you bring for us?"

Mama digs deep into our picnic basket. "This is what we will bring," she says, taking out a wad of bills so thick that Papa sucks in his breath.

The girl moves closer to me. She is staring at my skirt. "It's so pretty," she says.

"Thank you," I whisper.

Mama is busy counting out the money. The girl touches the red velvet material.

"It was a present from my aunt," I say.

The girl nods. "I like soft things," she whispers.

"Me too."

"Then I have something to show you." She leads me out toward the barn. "What's your name?" she asks.

"Juli."

"I'm Roza."

Her hair is blond and silky. I bet Mama wishes I had hair like that instead of my coarse curls. She wets my hair and pulls it straight with a big comb, but when it dries, it is as frizzy as ever.

I follow Roza to the back of the barn, and there in the hay is an orange cat with big yellow eyes. Roza reaches under the cat and takes out a tiny kitten.

"They're only two weeks old," she says.

It is the smallest kitten I have ever seen. I sit down cross-legged, and Roza puts him in my lap. His eyes are just starting to open, and his fur is short and fuzzy. I pet him between his ears with one finger.

"As soft as your skirt," Roza says.

"Softer," I say. "Is there only one?"

"There are six."

I can hardly believe that there are five more kittens underneath the mother. Roza takes out another, this one with gray and orange stripes. It opens its tiny mouth and yawns.

We take turns holding each kitten. Then Roza gives me all six to hold at once. They snuggle into each other and fall asleep. I wish I could stay with them forever.

"You want to take one home?" she asks. "They're too little now, but maybe in a few weeks."

"My parents won't let me," I say.

"Why not?"

"My mother says the city is no place for pets."

Roza nods. "I've never been to Budapest."

"Maybe you can visit me someday."

Roza is quiet for a minute, petting the kittens on my lap. "I don't think so. The train tickets cost too much. And besides that, I have to work."

"Work?"

Roza nods. "I have to clean the barn with my brothers, wash, iron, and, of course, make lace."

"I thought your mother made it."

"She does. We both do. Her eyes are getting old, you know, so she needs my help." Roza rubs her eyes. They look like mine when I stay up until three in the morning, reading.

"Your eyes are tired," I say.

Roza shrugs. "Most of the girls around here have bad eyes. It's from making such tiny stitches." She smiles. "But everyone says that soon I will be the best lace maker in our village."

"Really?"

Roza nods. "The only thing is, I'm too slow. 'Work faster,' my mother tells me. But if I make a mistake, she won't talk to me for the whole afternoon."

"My mother is like that too."

"She is?"

"She says I read too much and I slouch. She wants me to be the perfect young lady."

"But you already are the perfect young lady." Roza touches my velvet skirt and then looks up at my face. "At least you don't have eyes as red as a rabbit's."

One by one Roza puts the kittens back in the hay. Their mother licks them with her coarse tongue. They push their way underneath her belly. I've never seen an animal nurse before. The mother cat purrs as the kittens suck the milk from her nipples. Roza says we had better go back to the house.

Her mother and Mama are discussing the pattern that will be on my lace. Roza's mother suggests a raven in the middle. Mama thinks maybe a lion would be better. Lions are fierce, she says, and they symbolize the strength of the old Austro-Hungarian monarchy.

Roza's mother shakes her head. "Good luck. Isn't that what you want for a dowry?" She looks up toward the ceiling. "A raven with its wings spread carrying a ring in its mouth will be in the center."

Mama considers. She whispers something to Papa. I know he just wants to go home. "Yes, yes," he says. "Ravens are very smart and lucky birds."

The ladies look at each other. "I'll tell you what," Mama says. "Everyone says you are the best lace maker in all of Halas. We will leave the design up to you."

Roza's mother smiles, and I see that several of her teeth are missing. "I'll do my best," she says softly.

"Can we have kittens on my lace instead of a raven or a lion?" I ask.

Mama ignores me. "We're all set then, aren't we," she says. "We'll see you again in two months."

"Yes, Mrs. Kis," Roza's mother says. She is holding the stack of bills in her hand.

Roza's eyes meet mine. "See you soon," she says.

"Yes. I can't wait to see the kittens again," I say.

Roza nods. "They'll be big two months from now. You'll see."

The sun has come out and the fields are bright green all around. I look back; Roza is waving to me from the doorway. For a minute I wish I could stay here in Halas. I could lie in the middle of a big field of wheat and finish my book. I could sit with Roza in the barn and pet the kittens.

I follow Mama and Papa back to the station.

Chapter Four

We sit on the bench at the station and wait. The train is already a half hour late. Papa keeps looking at his watch.

"Juli," Mama says, "tell me the story again of the raven and the ring."

I sigh. "You know it."

"But I forgot some of the details."

"It will not hurt you to tell your mother the story," Papa says sternly.

I take a deep breath. "King Matthias was a very well loved king."

"When was that, Juli?"

"I think in 1400 or 1500. Around there."

"All right. That is close enough."

"King Matthias rewarded people who were generous and punished people who were stingy. He even disguised himself as a pauper to see how poor people were being treated."

"Go on," Mama says, taking two pieces of candy out of her purse and handing me one.

"For some reason that I forgot, King Matthias was imprisoned in Prague."

"Juli, when we get home, you can look in your Hungarian history book."

When I get home I will read about explorers, not about ancient kings and birds. But I keep my plans to myself.

"Now finish the story for us, Juli," Mama says.

"The king's mother was terribly worried about her son," I continue, "so she wrote a letter to him and asked her messengers to deliver it very quickly. One messenger said it would take six days. One said it would take three. The king's mother was upset because she needed the letter to be delivered quickly. Suddenly a raven appeared out of nowhere and snatched the letter out of her hand. Then, a day later, the same bird brought a response from Prague. King Matthias was still alive."

"But what about the ring? Didn't the lace maker say she would put a raven with a ring in the middle of the tablecloth?"

I shrug. "I don't know anything about the ring."

Mama pokes Papa. "Why a ring and not a letter?" she asks him.

"A ring is more beautiful than a letter," Papa says.

"You're right," Mama says.

"I would rather have a kitten than a raven," I say.

Finally we hear the rumbling of the train.

I wipe the window with my sleeve.

"Juli, how can you use your blouse for a rag?" Mama scolds.

"The window is dirty."

Papa hands me a piece of newspaper, and I wipe the glass as well as I can. The flat plains have changed into gentle hills with farmhouses and barns. Cows dot the hillsides. Mama hated living in the countryside, but I would love to live at Roza's with the kittens. I like the striped one. He licked my hand with his rough tongue. He tried to suck on my baby finger. And when he opened his mouth, just the tiniest little sound came out. I want to ask Mama and Papa if I can have the striped kitten when he gets bigger, but I know what they'll say. *A city is no place for a pet.* Mama doesn't want to get cat hair on the furniture and on my clothes. She doesn't want me to go to school smelling like a zoo.

"You negotiated very well for the price of the lace," Papa says.

Mama nods.

"How long have you been saving?" Papa asks.

"Twelve years," Mama says, patting my arm. "On the day our Juli was born, I started saving a little here, a little there."

Papa nods.

"Mama."

"Yes, Juli."

"Can I have one of Roza's kittens?"

"Who is Roza?"

"The lace maker's daughter."

"Juli, the city is—"

I feel my eyes tear up. Why did I bother to ask? Mama never cares what I think.

"I'm never getting married," I say. I have spoken so loudly that the young man sitting across the aisle turns his head.

"Juli—"

"I'm not," I say firmly. "Ever."

Mama puts her lips together tightly and stares out the window. Papa puts his hand on her knee.

Chapter Five

Late in the afternoon Papa and I head to the corner to find Lajos Bacsi and Sari. "What took you so long?" Lajos Bacsi asks. "We were about to leave, weren't we, Sarika?"

She nods.

"We had business to attend to," Papa says. "In Halas."

Lajos Bacsi lifts his eyebrows.

"A dowry," Papa whispers.

Lajos Bacsi smiles at me. "For little Juli? Already? I thought that in the city these days— Never mind. It's never too early to think ahead," he says, setting up the chessboard.

"You sound like my wife," Papa says.

"I want a gold necklace for my dowry," Sari says, "with earrings to match." She prances around the table like a princess.

"I don't want a dowry," I say.

"Why not?"

"People in Budapest don't have dowries."

"Some do and some don't," Papa says.

"Most people don't," I say.

Papa is busy with the chess pieces.

"Anyway, I'm not getting married," I say.

Sari stops prancing and holds on to the table. "You're not? I'm marrying Andras."

"Your brother Andras?"

"Of course."

"You can't marry your brother."

Sari is prancing again. "Well, then, I'll marry Zoli."

"Who's Zoli?"

"My cousin."

Sari is making me dizzy.

"So, if you're not getting married, what are you going to do?" she asks. Her skinny legs are going faster and faster around the table.

"Sari, stop running," Lajos Bacsi says.

"But I'm a horse," she says.

"Not in the café," her uncle says.

Sari plops down in the chair. "Are you going to be a nurse?" she asks me.

"No."

"What, then?"

I don't know what to say. Sari's only eight, but she has her plans. I have no idea what I want to do. The only thing I know is that I want to have a cat.

"I'm going to live on a farm," I say.

"With a farmer?"

"I'll be the farmer."

Sari makes a sad face. "Those people are so poor," she says.

"How do you know?"

"Don't you see them at the market, Juli? All those ladies with scarves around their heads carrying baskets of peppers? Is that the kind of farmer lady you mean?"

I wish Sari would stop her chattering. I should have stayed home and finished my book. "Maybe I'll be a veterinarian. I'll be a veterinarian who lives on a farm and helps sick animals."

Sari's face lights up. "Now I see."

Lajos Bacsi and Papa have captured lots of chess pieces. Sari picks up two pawns and says they are both in love with the queen. How will she choose? "What makes it especially hard," she says, "is that they look the same." She moves them around on the sidewalk. "Hey, Juli, how will she choose?"

I shrug.

"I know. She'll see which one is stronger." Sari smiles up at me. "Here, Juli, you can have the horse, since you like animals."

I take it, but I don't feel like playing with Sari.

"Here. The pawn can ride on the horse."

She doesn't need me to make up her stories. "I'm going home," I say.

"Already? I waited for you for so long."

Her eyes are pleading, but I tell her my stomach hurts, which is sort of true. I still feel like I'm bumping up and down on the train. Sari walks with me part of the way up the hill. She slips her hand in mine.

"I hope your stomach ache goes away," she says, "and if it does, you can come back."

"All right."

"Hey, Juli, you could be a veterinarian and still get married."

"I don't want to." My voice comes out so sharp that it startles me.

Chapter Six

Mama is shelling peas in the kitchen. I go right to my room, shut the door, and open my book. The poor dogs have to pull the sleds in temperatures of fifty degrees below zero with particles of snow hurtling into their eyes. I especially like the husky named Buss. No matter how hard it is, he never stops pulling. There is a pencil drawing of him with his head cocked and his ears up. Then, finally, Byrd has to shoot many of the dogs in order to save food. Tears come to my eyes. Couldn't he have done something to keep Buss?

Suddenly I'm worried about Roza's kittens. A fox could come into the barn at night and kill them all. There would be nothing the mother cat could do. Or they could get sick and die. They are so tiny.

Mama opens the door. "Juli, don't read on your bed. Sit straight in the chair. Or better yet, come and help me in the kitchen. Too much reading will ruin your eyes. Then you will need glasses like an old librarian; can you imagine how that will be?"

"What will you do with the lace tablecloth if I don't get married?" I ask.

Mama ignores my question. "At least, Juli, turn on the light."

"Will you sell it?"

"Juli, what are you talking about?"

"I want to know how much money we can get for the lace tablecloth."

"It will never be for sale."

"But if we decided to sell it, how much could we get?"

"Juli, stop."

The words keep coming. "I told you, I don't need a dowry. Roza's eyes are all red from making the lace. Her mother can hardly see. I'll sell the lace and give them the money."

"And do you think that if we don't order the lace, their eyes will improve? Did you see the money I gave them, Juli? Did you? With that they can fix the barn, buy another cow, whatever they need."

"There is nothing wrong with their barn. Inside is a mother cat with six kittens and you won't let me have even one. Someday I'll live on a farm like Roza."

"Don't talk nonsense."

Now I am shouting. "Why don't you ever listen to me?"

"You have no idea what you are talking about, Juli. Living on a farm is not at all what you think." Mama's face is red. "It's work from sunrise to sunset, that's what it is, and for all that work, a few turnips." Mama turns away.

"But Roza has—"

We hear the door of the apartment open, and Papa is there. "What's going on here?"

I look down. Mama opens her mouth like she is about to say something, but then she leans on Papa and they shuffle out of my room.

Outside my window the street is dark except for a glow around the streetlights. In Halas there are no streetlights. I bet they can see so many stars. I wonder if Roza and her mother are working on my lace with the light from a candle. It must be so cozy in their small room with candles and bobbins of white thread.

Mama is crying. I hear Papa's deep voice trying to comfort her, but I can't understand the words. I wonder what Papa is saying. That I am a silly girl? That I don't mean what I say? That I am a twelve-year-old baby? I can go into the living room and hug Mama and tell her that I'll be a better daughter from now on. She'll stroke my frizzy hair and rub my back. But my legs feel like lead.

I sit at my desk and take out a clean sheet of paper. *Dear Mama,* I write, *I'm sorry that I behaved so badly.* But then what? I can't take back my words. Anyway, no matter what Mama thinks, I don't want a dowry. Why do I have to have a mother who is so old-fashioned? The ink makes a big blot in the center of my paper. I turn it into the nose of a cat and add two squinting eyes and two ears. But I've never been good at drawing. I tear the paper into small pieces and open my book.

Admiral Byrd and his men built a place called Little America and survived for many months in the bitter cold. But I wonder suddenly if it was worth it. Why would anyone even want to go to the South Pole? Once they got there, then what? They put up a flag and that was all. The dogs were not given a choice about whether to go. They were not given a choice about withstanding freezing temperatures only to get killed. I move my eyes quickly across the words on the pages, and soon I am done with the book.

My stomach is growling, but I don't want to leave my room. What will I say to Mama? She didn't call me for dinner. My stomach drops. What will I do if Mama is done worrying about me?

I wish I still had my book to read. Or another one. I wish I had Mama's dowry money so I could go to the bookstore and buy all the books I want. I pull a book of poems by Arany Janos off my shelf. It was a gift from my last year's Hungarian teacher. In the front he wrote, *To Juli, you are a wonderful student. Thank you for all your hard work. You will go far. Yours, Mr. Kemenyi.* What does it mean to go far? Far like the South Pole? I open the book to a random spot in the middle, and there is the famous poem about King Matthias.

Maybe next time we go to Halas, I can show the poem to Roza. I'll copy it for her. I write the title, *The Mother of King Matthias,* in my best handwriting. Then I start copying the verses:

Szilagyi Erzsebet
swiftly wrote a letter;

it was moist
with loving tears
many, too, and bitter.

For her son
held in Prague,
were these fair words she
wrote
harshly kept
in prison cell;
good news to him it
brought.

The door opens, and there is Mama. "Are you hungry, Juli?" she asks. Her voice is hoarse.

I nod.

"Come."

I cover the poem with a blank sheet of paper and follow my mother into the kitchen. I eat my bread and soup quickly without saying a word.

Chapter Seven

When we go to Halas in September, the design for my lace is all planned out. Roza's mother has drawn it with pencil on onion-skin paper. In the middle is a raven with its wings spread. Around it are cherry trees and flowers. Then around that are squares with the lions Mama wanted, each one carrying a crown in its paws, and ravens with rings in their beaks. Roza's mother has already started making the first square.

Mama is so pleased. Roza's mother is smiling too, but her eyes look worse than I remembered. They are pink around the edges with a yellow crust in the corners. She dabs at them with a handkerchief.

Roza and I head out to the barn. The kittens' eyes are open. Roza has named the striped one Bobbin. "He's the naughty one," she says, stroking him under his chin. "He came into our house and got into our bobbins of thread. My mother almost killed him, she was so mad. Now I make sure he stays out here in the barn."

Bobbin climbs onto my lap. I pet his back, and he flexes his paws on my stockings. Then he curls up into a ball on my skirt.

"He doesn't usually like to be held," Roza says. "He must like you. Did you ask your mother if you could have a kitten?"

"The answer was the same as it always is."

"How about we hide him in your lunch basket?"

I shake my head. "She'd notice."

"How about inside your jacket?"

"He'll meow. Mama will hear him."

Roza rubs her eyes.

"Are you tired?" I ask.

"Not really. Just my eyes are sore."

"From making the lace?"

Roza nods.

"I told my mother I don't need a dowry. I told her it's all a waste."

Roza looks up quickly. Her blue eyes are open wide. "You mean you don't want the lace?"

"No, the lace is very beautiful. What I mean is that I don't need a dowry. I'm never getting married anyway."

Roza is quiet. I'm sorry I said anything about not wanting the lace. She stands up, gets a pitchfork, and starts moving fresh hay over to where the cat sleeps. Bobbin is purring loudly. Roza does not look over at us.

"Sorry," I whisper.

Roza keeps moving the hay.

"Do you want me to help you?" I ask.

Finally she stops working. "I'll tell my mother that you don't need a dowry."

"Please don't. I love the Halas lace. I just don't want—" My voice cracks. "I just don't want your eyes to get red and crusty like your mother's."

Roza sits down next to me again. With her finger, she draws circles in the dirt on the barn floor. "You know, my mother says she's never worked on a tablecloth as beautiful as yours."

"Really?"

"She showed the design to some of our neighbors. They said they will help with the edging. And with the money we earn, we'll get another cow and sell the milk and cheese."

"I wish I could stay here and help you on the farm."

Roza looks out the barn door at her brother. He is carrying tools for their father. The muscles in his skinny arms are bulging, and he staggers under the weight of the tools. "I don't think you would like it," she says softly.

"Why not?"

Roza is quiet for a minute. "There is nothing here for a girl from Budapest." She swallows hard. "We have one small school that goes until sixth grade. We don't have electricity in our houses. We don't have any theater or concerts. Have you ever seen a movie?"

I nod. "My aunt Zsofi takes me sometimes."

"You're lucky," Roza says softly.

Bobbin stands and stretches. I stroke his silky fur. "But you are so lucky to have the kittens."

"I asked my mother about putting a kitten in the lace," Roza says.

"What did she say?"

"The same thing your mother said when you asked if you could have a real one."

Roza is drawing in the dirt. I see the body of a cat, arched in a stretch. Then comes the head, the ears, the tail. "How do you do that?" I ask, impressed.

Roza shrugs. "I like to draw. Just like my mama, I guess." She erases the cat and draws another one. This one is curled into a ball like Bobbin's mother.

"Perfect," I say.

"I practice a lot," she says, erasing that one too.

Then I stand up and take the poem I copied out of my pocket. "Here. I brought something for you."

Roza sounds the title out slowly and stumbles over the first verse. Her neck and cheeks turn red. "I'm a very poor reader," she says, looking down so that her blond hair hides her face. "I miss school when we have to finish a lace collar or a set of coasters or a centerpiece. The teacher put me back with the second graders." Roza's eyes are teary. "Everyone laughs because I can't even spell as well as the first graders."

I touch her arm. "Here. I'll read the poem out loud to you." Roza shuts her eyes, and I read all twelve verses.

"It's beautiful," she says when I am finished. "My grandmother told me that story, but the poem is like music."

Then we notice that her brothers have been listening. "Can you read it again?" the taller one asks.

When I'm finished the second time, the younger one says, "That's the same story that's in Mama's new lace."

"I'll leave the poem here so you can read it whenever you want to."

Roza shakes her head. "You saw. I can't read it."

"Maybe I can," the older boy says. He takes the paper and reads the first verse slowly but clearly.

Mama is calling.

"Next time I come, we'll practice again," I tell Roza.

She looks at her brother. "Give Juli back the poem."

"No, you keep it," I say. "I copied it for you."

Chapter Eight

The November rain is cold and icy. Mama wraps me tightly in a shawl, a sweater, and my warmest wool coat. I feel like a stuffed goose. "Better a stuffed goose than a sore throat," she says.

When we get to Roza's, I knock but nobody answers. Mama looks at me and knocks louder. Finally Roza opens the door softly and puts her finger to her lips. "My mother is sleeping," she says.

We tiptoe into the room. The bed has been moved closer to the stove, and Roza's mother looks shrunken underneath the thick comforter.

"What's the matter?" Mama whispers.

"First my mother said just her eyes hurt, but then she got a terrible headache," Roza explains. "My father went to get the doctor. He will come soon." Her face falls. "Mama told me to tell you that the fourth square is not yet done. No need to leave the money." Roza's voice is hoarse. "I tried to finish it last night, but I made a mistake and had to take out so many stitches."

She leads us to a corner of the room. The picture of the flying raven has been retraced in blue ink. The paper is stretched in an embroidery frame, and the design has been outlined in white thread. "I tried to get the whole picture tacked down last night," Roza says. "I thought that this morning Mama and I could start filling in the wings, but I overslept and Mama is not well." Roza rubs her eyes. "But when you come in January, I'll have everything ready."

Roza's mother shifts in the bed and lifts her head. "I'm sorry," she says, "for the delay." She talks with her eyes closed. Roza brings her a washcloth for her forehead.

Mama sits down on the edge of the bed and takes Roza's mother's hand in hers. "Would you like a drink of water?" she asks.

Roza and I slip out to the barn. The kittens are so big I can hardly believe it. Two of them are wrestling in the hay. A third is climbing up the rafters. Bobbin comes right to me and rubs on my legs. I sit down, and he crawls into my lap, shuts his eyes, and purrs.

"You're so lucky. You can play with the kittens whenever you want," I say to Roza. I put my cheek on Bobbin's warm fur and feel his whole body vibrating as he purrs.

"Not really," says Roza. "I have to work on the lace for at least two hours every day. Then I have to feed the chickens, help my brothers clean the barn, stoke the stove, and start the soup."

"What about school?"

"I stopped going," Roza says.

"You did?"

Roza blushes. "Sorry, Juli. I didn't practice reading the poem." She takes it out of a small bag hanging off a nail in the wall of the barn. "Here. You can take it home."

"But it's yours. Or maybe your brother wants it."

Roza shoves the paper into my pocket. "We don't need it," she says.

Suddenly I wish I had never come to Halas. Roza doesn't want me here in her barn with her kittens. She doesn't want the poem I copied for her. And I don't want her lace either. What am I doing more than a hundred kilometers from home in a freezing barn?

I stand up and Bobbin jumps off my lap.

"Where are you going?" Roza asks.

"To find my mother," I say.

"Wait." Roza reaches into the bag again. "I have something for you." She hands me a piece of paper. On it she has drawn a perfect likeness of Bobbin. "I thought you might want this so you can remember him." She reaches down to pet Bobbin. "My father says we have to give the kittens away this spring."

"Why so soon?"

"Look how big they are. Soon they won't even be kittens."

"Who are you going to give them to?"

"I don't know. Another farmer, if we can find one."

"And if not?"

"Then my father will just let them go." Roza swallows hard.

I don't know what to say. The air in the barn is so cold we

can see our breath. "Thanks. Thanks for the picture," I say finally.

Bobbin has gone to rejoin his brothers and sisters in the hay. They are huddled together to stay warm. I can't imagine Bobbin alone in a new barn.

Roza touches my arm. "Hey, Juli, since I'm not going to school anymore, do you think you could teach me when you come?"

"Teach you what?"

"All the things you learn. I bet you're the smartest one in the class."

"I do well enough, but I hate school."

"Why?"

"The others call me 'teacher's pet' and 'giraffe.' Just because I know the answers, they hate me. At snack time, they won't share with me. 'We don't have hay for giraffes,' they say."

"I wish I could go to school with you. Then we could share our snacks." Roza shivers. "Sorry about the poem. I didn't have time to practice. Because of Mama."

"The doctor will come soon."

Roza nods. "Last time he told Mama not to strain her eyes, but no matter how often I remind her, she doesn't listen."

"It's because of my lace," I whisper.

"No. It's because we are the lace makers of Halas," Roza says firmly.

Chapter Nine

When I arrive at school on Monday, Agi is whispering by the fence with Kata and Baba. They are looking at me and laughing. I try to get by without speaking to them, but Kata is blocking my path.

"So, Juli, we hear the wedding date is set."

I try to walk past, but the three girls are in my way.

"Who's the lucky man?" Baba asks.

I don't answer.

"Say something," Kata demands.

"I don't know what you are talking about," I say finally. I wish I could catch Agi's eye. Sometimes we read the same books and talk about them. She came over to my apartment after school once last year. But she is looking down at her feet.

"Of course you know," says Baba. "How can a girl get a dowry without having a husband in mind?"

The blood rushes to my face. How do they know? Who could have told them about the lace? Sari's older cousin walks past and winks at me. Suddenly I know what must have happened.

Kata and Baba are humming the kissing song. They put in the names of various boys and watch my expression.

"She smiled, did you see?" Kata says after they put in Laszlo.

"Let's try Istvan," says Baba.

They sing the song again.

"I say it's Laszlo," says Kata. She turns to Agi. "What do you think?"

Agi nods. "Must be."

The bell rings, and we head toward the classroom. I am the very last one in.

In the afternoon we have Hungarian grammar and writing with my favorite teacher. She hands back our dictation from last week. I have a perfect "1" at the top of my paper. Kata glances over and rolls her eyes.

Today we are to write a paragraph about our goals for the upcoming year. The problem is that I don't really have any. I want to go someplace far away from the girls in my class. I remember the words in the front of my Arany Janos book: *You will go far.* I'd like to fly over the Danube like the raven. I'd like to explore Antarctica like Admiral Byrd. I'd like to be a veterinarian and live on a farm with lots of kittens. But these are goals for my life, not goals for this year.

Kata pokes me from behind. "Write about *him*," she says, giggling.

"Describe the wedding plans," Baba says.

I try to scoot forward on my bench, but my legs are so long that they hardly fit into the small space. This is all Mama's fault. She's the one with the old-fashioned country ideas. If we had never gone to Halas for the lace, Kata and Baba and Agi would not be bothering me. But then, if we hadn't gone, I would never have met Roza.

The teacher is walking up and down the rows. I have to start. I write about Roza and how I plan to visit her and her family often this year. I describe their one-room house and the barn with the kittens. I write about the pattern for the lace and the red eyes of the lace makers. The only thing I don't write is that the lace tablecloth is for my dowry. I write so fast that I'm surprised when the class period is over.

"You had a lot to say about him, didn't you, Juli," Kata says, sliding past me to link arms with Baba and Agi.

On the way home from school, my head is spinning. Maybe I'm hungry. But my stomach is churning.

"What's the matter?" Mama asks the moment she sees me. She touches my forehead and strokes my cheek. "Juliska, you are as hot as an oven." Mama's hands are cool and dry. She leads me to my bed.

I shiver under my quilt. I want to read *Oliver Twist*, but the words are blurry on the page.

"Rest, now, Juli, rest," Mama says, taking the book from my hands.

•

When I wake up, it's dark in my room. Mama and Papa are both there, talking in low voices. "Don't worry," Papa says. "Look, she's better already. You'll see, by morning the fever will break."

Mama is touching my head. "But feel. She is still so warm."

Papa is touching me too. "She's sweating. That's the best thing for a fever."

I want to talk, but my throat is on fire. Papa holds a cup of water to my lips. I try to take a sip, but how can I swallow?

"See, Mama, she's drinking a little," Papa says.

"Yes," Mama says. "A little." Then they are quiet, but I know they are still there, sitting next to each other on the edge of my bed.

I dream about Roza and her family. They keep calling for the doctor, but he won't come. I say, *I am a doctor*, but nobody can hear me. When I wake up, I am shouting.

"What is it, Juli?" Papa asks.

"They're blind."

"Shhh, Juli, you had a bad dream," Papa says.

"I kept saying that I was a doctor, but nobody believed me."

"Shhh, Juli, don't worry. We can hear you now."

Mama tiptoes in with a cool washcloth for my forehead.

"She's a little better," Papa says softly.

Chapter Ten

When we go in January, I take a notebook and pencil for Roza. At home, before we went, I made up a simple story about a naughty kitten who tangles the thread, and I wrote it on the first page of the notebook. I left room between the sentences so Roza can practice copying them.

At the house, Roza's mother is sitting in a chair by the window working on the sixth square. She has taken it out of the embroidery frame and is stitching it on her lap with a fine needle.

"How are you?" Mama asks, kneeling next to the chair.

Roza's mother smiles a little. "Better, thank you. Not well, but better."

"There's a bad flu going around. Juli caught it too, but you know children. One week in bed and then she was fine."

Roza's mother sighs. "I wish I could say the same."

"Maybe with spring, you will regain your strength."

"My strength, yes. But I'm not sure about my eyes." Roza's mother is working on the lace with her eyes almost shut. She feels the stitches with her fingertips.

Mama takes out a wad of money, but Roza's mother turns away. "We are behind schedule," she says, "so I can understand if you would like to withhold payment."

"No matter," Mama says, setting the bills on the table.

Roza's mother stops stitching and looks down. "Thank you," she says. "You are a very good woman." Then she shows Mama the flower pattern she has designed for the border of the tablecloth. "Lilies of the valley. You know, the small pearl flower that comes out in early spring. My favorite."

"Mine too," Mama says. She touches the tiny white stitches. "It's gorgeous," she says.

"Please, is Roza here?" I ask.

"In the barn," her mother says.

I slip out the door and go to the barn. Roza doesn't see me at first. She is shouting at her brother. "You are so lazy!" she tells him. "Why don't you do what I tell you?"

"I do," he says softly.

I have never seen Roza like this before. She stamps her foot. "Finish cleaning the stall right now."

"But I'm tired."

"You had better listen to me or I'll tell Papa."

The boy picks up a pitchfork that looks heavier than he is.

"Hurry up."

When Roza sees me, she covers her mouth with her hand. "I didn't know you were here," she says. "We have work to do."

I should leave—go back to the house and wait for Mama. But before I do, Roza steps closer. "Sorry," she says softly. "I shouldn't yell at him. But if I don't, he sits in the barn and daydreams."

I watch her brother moving the hay. "The pitchfork is too heavy."

She shrugs. "He'll get stronger."

"Do you still have all the kittens?"

Roza points to a corner of the barn. "Now Papa says we can keep one of the kittens, but I can't decide which one."

Bobbin comes over and rubs against my legs. "How about Bobbin?"

"I don't know. He likes you best, but the white one likes me."

"Then keep the white one."

"I can't decide."

"I like this one," her brother says, bringing over the orange kitten.

"Papa says it's my decision," Roza says, ignoring her brother.

I always wished I had a younger sibling, but when I see Roza with her brother, I am not so sure. She talks to him the way Kata and Baba talk to me. Finally he leaves us alone in the barn.

"Hey, I brought you something," I say, handing the notebook to Roza. She turns to the first page and moves her eyes over the words.

"I don't have time to practice."

I shrug. "You can keep it. Just in case."

"Anyway, there's no need for a girl to learn how to write," Roza says, closing the notebook.

"Who told you that?"

"My father."

"That is a very old-fashioned idea."

Roza pulls her eyebrows together. "My father is not old-fashioned."

Then we are quiet. I shouldn't have said anything about Roza's father. But how can she think that there is no reason for her to read and write?

The kittens are walking around us. They are almost as big as their mother. Bobbin sniffs my boots, and I can see his breath in the cold air. Finally he settles on my lap.

"Sorry," I whisper to Roza.

Roza sighs. "I'm sorry too. Mama says I'm mean to everybody these days. I don't even know why." She rubs her eyes with the back of her hand. The white kitten lies down in the hay, and she pets him between his ears.

"I want to show you something," Roza says finally. She climbs up on a rafter, brings down a small cloth bag, and dumps the contents onto her lap. At first I'm not sure what it is. Then I see a piece of white fabric with an outline in thicker white thread. Two ears, a long body, a thin tail. I suck in my breath. There in beautiful white lace is a cat. "This way, even after we give most of the kittens away, I can remember them in my lace."

"When do you have time?"

"Early in the morning, when everyone is asleep, I play with the kittens and stitch for a few minutes. Hey, Juli, do you want me to teach you how?"

"I'm not good at things like that. In our domestic skills class, I'm terrible."

"It's not that hard, really. Here. First you outline the shape with the thicker thread, and then you fill in the spaces with a small pattern. See this one? I made it up myself."

Roza's hands move so quickly that I can't see what she is doing.

"Do you want to try?"

"I don't know."

"Come on. I'll help you." She shows me where to put the needle. I draw the thread through slowly, but it forms a knot in back that Roza has to fix.

I hand the project back to her. "I'm not good at handiwork."

"But you could practice at home."

I shake my head. "You don't have time to practice writing, and I don't have time to practice stitching."

Roza moves her hands like lightning as we talk. She asks me about school.

"Now the other girls are teasing me again."

"Why?"

"Because of my dowry."

"What is there to tease about?"

"They think it's funny that I'm only twelve and getting a dowry already."

"I don't see what's funny about that. My aunt started a dowry for my cousin when she was born, and then when she turned fifteen, she got married."

"In Budapest, people don't have dowries."

"You mean they get married with nothing?"

"I think when they get engaged, they order all kinds of things from the big boutiques on Vaci Street."

Roza is thinking. "I bet the girls at school are just jealous. Sometimes girls in the village laugh at me about my red eyes, but Mama says they're just jealous because I can make lace better than they can."

"The girls at school hate me. That's all. They sing a kissing song and put in the names of all these boys."

"I bet now you really wish you didn't have a lace dowry."

I'm quiet for a minute, watching Roza's hands pulling the needle. "No, I don't wish that. I like coming to Halas to visit you and the kittens. I only wish that the girls at school would leave me alone."

Mama is calling. I stand up quickly, and Bobbin jumps to the ground. "See you soon," I say.

"Thanks for the notebook. I'll try to practice."

Chapter Eleven

The snow gets so high in February that Mama doesn't want to go to Halas. "But Mama, the trains are still running," I say.

"And what if there is a blizzard and we are stuck in Halas?"

"Then we can sleep at Roza's."

"Where in one small room would we sleep?"

"On quilts on the floor."

Mama shakes her head. "And what about school?"

"I'd just have to miss a day. Anyway, I'm ahead of everyone else. All I do all day is read."

"Juli, we are not going in this snow."

"What about Roza's family? They are counting on the money."

"I sent it yesterday by the post."

"But Mama, Roza is waiting for me."

"Roza is far too busy to sit around and wait for anyone, unlike you who have time to spare."

"How do you know if she is waiting for me or not?"

Mama opens her eyes wide. "How do I know? Because I lived on a farm and I woke up at four in the morning to feed the fire and make the breakfast and sweep the floor." She shakes her head. "How do I know."

"But that doesn't mean that Roza is not waiting for me."

Mama shuts her lips tight. Papa starts to say something about how the weather might improve tomorrow, but Mama takes her teacup and leaves the room before he has finished his sentence.

Snow is falling in big, heavy flakes that are piling up on the windowsill. I go into my room and sit at my desk. Mama thinks that one farm is like the next. She thinks that just because she didn't like living in the countryside, nobody does. But she doesn't know Roza. I take out the drawing Roza gave me. The cat's tail is so perfect, up in the air, waving. I sit at my desk and write a letter in printed letters. If I make the sentences simple, she'll be able to read it, I am sure.

> *Dear Roza,*
>
> *I'm so sorry we can't come to see you. The snow is too deep and Mama doesn't want to take the train. How's your mother doing? How are you? How are all the kittens? They must be completely grown up by now. Do you still have all of them? I love the picture you gave me. I think it is Bobbin. Please write back. Don't worry about spelling.*
> *Love,*
> *Juli*

On the bottom of the paper I try to draw a picture of a cat, but it looks very stiff and blockish. I want to erase it, but the pencil smudges. I put the letter into an envelope and address it to Voros Roza, Halas, Hungary. Then at the bottom I write in parentheses, *The Best Lace Makers in the World*, and I head out to the mailbox.

The snow is almost to the top of my boots. Everything is so quiet that I can hear myself breathe. I wonder what Halas looks like covered in snow. The muddy roads would be clean and white. The small slope behind the barn would be perfect for sledding. But Roza might not have time to go sledding. She might not have a sled. I hope the kittens are warm inside the barn.

I drop the letter into the mailbox and turn to go home. There, crouched underneath the mailbox, is a striped gray and orange cat. I take off my mittens and pet his silky fur. He stands and rubs against my legs. I look into his eyes. Could it be Bobbin? Bobbin had the same kind of striped tail and white paws, but I can't remember, were his eyes so yellow? Could a cat make it all the way from Halas to Budapest? Could he have walked so far? It doesn't seem possible. Maybe one day he got onto the train at the station. But where would he have hidden?

The cat looks up at me with his wide-open eyes and meows. "Sorry, Kitty, I can't take you home," I say, but when I walk, he comes right behind me, jumping from one boot print to the next. Every few steps I turn around, and he is still following me. When I open the front door of my building, he slips into the stairwell.

Mama has several fabric swatches on the kitchen table. "Come, Juli, tell me which one you like." There is a yellow velvet, a pink brocade, and several blue satin fabrics.

"What for?" I ask.

"A dress," Mama says. "I told Mari Neni that we would make a selection, and then she will sew it for you."

"I already have plenty of dresses," I say.

"But you need something a little more dressy now that you are almost thirteen."

"I have the red velvet skirt."

"A skirt is a skirt and a dress is a dress." Mama holds the yellow velvet up close to my face. "I think this one will do nicely," she says.

As usual, Mama has already decided. All I can think of is that the yellow matches Bobbin's eyes. I want to go out and pet him, but Mama will ask me what I am doing in the drafty stairwell.

When I go to bed, I can't stop thinking about the cat. It could just be one that looks like Bobbin. After all, there are lots of cats with striped tails and white paws. But maybe, somehow, Bobbin did make his way to Budapest.

Maybe he is cold. He must miss his brothers and sisters and mother and Roza. Mama and Papa are in their room. The light is off. I tiptoe to the front door and turn the key in the lock so softly that it doesn't even make a click.

The stairwell is dim, and for a minute I can't see anything. Bobbin or not, that's what I'll call him. He winds himself around my legs. I sit down, and he crawls onto my nightgown and purrs so loudly that I'm afraid Mama and Papa might hear. "Shhh, Bobbin Kitty, it really is you," I whisper, scratching him under his neck. He shuts his eyes and keeps on purring.

Maybe Bobbin is trying to tell me something. Maybe he is a messenger, like the raven in my lace. But what has he come to say? I stroke his back. There, hanging from the end of his tail, is a small piece of white thread. I look at it closely in the dim light. It could be any thread, but I think it looks like the linen thread that Roza uses. I put my face into Bobbin's fur. "Thank you for coming," I whisper.

When I am able to tear myself away, I go to the kitchen and pour a little bit of milk into a container. I carry it carefully out to the stairwell. Bobbin stretches, rubs against my legs, tests the milk with his paw, and then starts lapping at it with his tongue.

"Good night, Bobbin Kitty," I tell him. "Sleep well."

The sun is shining on the sparkling white snow when I wake up. People are already out shoveling off the sidewalk. I see Bobbin outside leaping playfully in the snowdrifts. How did he get out? What will he do in a big city like Budapest? He might not know that the streetcars are dangerous. Maybe I should take him back to Halas. But then, maybe this is where he wants to be.

Chapter Twelve

I have written several letters to Roza, but she never writes back. I tell her how Bobbin stays in the stairwell and comes out only when Mama and Papa are either asleep or not home. I tell her how he plays with the ends of my braids. I tell her that the girls at school have been ignoring me, thank God, so I have a lot of time to read. I tell her that Mama and I have been staying out of each other's way most of the time. I ask her to write me back. Even if she can't spell the words right, I tell her, I'll be able to understand them. At the end I write, *PS I can't wait to see you in March.*

But the first Saturday in March, Mama says she is going to Halas alone. She has enrolled me in Saturday afternoon dancing lessons.

"Dancing lessons? Who says I want to go to dancing lessons?" I ask.

"Juli, you have to learn at least the basics. Here you are, almost a teenager, and you don't know the slightest thing about how to behave at a party."

"I'm not going," I say, crossing my arms.

"Juli, the yellow dress is ready; remember the fabric we picked? Many of your classmates will be there. I'm sure you'll have a good time."

"I'm going to see Roza," I shout, stomping my foot. "And nobody can make me go to a dance class."

Mama tries to pat my arm. "Juli, this obsession you have with Roza and the farm has to end. Roza is a nice girl, but she is not company for you. How about Agi? I bet she'll be at the dance lesson too."

Now I know that Mama planned the dance lesson precisely to keep me from going to Halas. First she says I have to go, and then she says I can't. Tears are streaming down my face. So, Roza is not good enough for me. Mama prefers Kata and Baba and Agi, who laugh at me and sing kissing songs.

Mama grabs the lunch basket and runs out of the apartment. From the stairwell she shouts, "Papa, make sure to get her there on time. Two o'clock, St. Stephen Street."

Mama's high-heeled shoes tap loudly as she goes down the stairs, and then the door clicks shut. I run to my room and bury my face in my quilt. Mama never listens. Not to me, not to Papa, not to anyone. If only I had my own money. Then I could buy my own ticket to Halas. Lajos Bacsi gave me one pengo for my birthday, and I found one more on the streetcar, but two pengo is not nearly enough for a train ticket. I could sell something. But what? I could work for money. Pali from downstairs shovels snow, and people pay him. But Mama would never let me shovel snow, not in a million years.

Papa knocks on my door. "Juli, I'm going to play chess. Will you come with me?"

I consider for a minute. Lajos Bacsi always makes me laugh with his silly jokes and twinkling eyes. But today I don't feel like listening to jokes and Sari's endless chatter. "No," I tell him.

Papa stands outside the door for a minute. "Are you sure?"

"Yes."

"I'll be back in about an hour."

I hear Papa walk to the door. He stops. "Juli, if you change your mind, just come on down," he calls back. Then he is gone.

Papa lets me decide what I want to do and what I don't. Why can't Mama be more that way? Why does she treat me like a baby?

When I am sure Papa is past the corner, I go to the stairwell and let Bobbin into the apartment. He explores my desk. He bats a pencil onto the floor and chases it around the room. He pounces on my feet.

I sit down at my desk and start a letter to Roza. I tell her I'm sorry I couldn't come this time, but I will surely come in May. I tell her that Bobbin is doing very well. *Do you want me to bring him back when I come?* I ask. After I write that, tears come to my eyes again. Then I add, *I hope he is happy here in Budapest, even though I'm not.*

I fold the letter and put it into an envelope, but I don't feel like walking to the mailbox. Why should I mail it anyway? Why write letters to somebody who never writes back? Maybe Roza doesn't even get my letters. Maybe her eyes have gotten worse like her mother's and she can't see my small handwriting. I should have written in big printed letters. She's just learning to read. Maybe that's the problem. Or maybe she's still mad about what I said about her father. Maybe she ignores my letters as she does her little brother's soft voice.

I sort through the papers on my desk. There's the composition I wrote about Roza's farm. I ball up the paper and throw it onto the floor. Bobbin bats it with his dainty paws. Then I lie down on my bed and pick up a new book that my teacher lent me. It's a biography of Marie Curie. When Marie was a little girl in Poland, she taught herself to read. Her parents wanted her to play like other children with dolls and toys, but she kept on reading anything she could find. Then when she grew up, she didn't care what everybody else thought. She just forged ahead with her ideas even when other people thought they were stupid.

Bobbin jumps onto the bed and settles on my stomach. I close my eyes and stroke his fur. I want to be like Marie Curie. I want to make new discoveries. But discoveries about what? Or I can be like Admiral Byrd. I want to find new places. I want to decide things for myself. I want to live far away from Mama so she can't make me wear a yellow dress and go to dance lessons.

I glance at the clock. Papa will be back soon. I pick Bobbin up, put him into the stairwell, and go back to my book. Marie Curie and her husband are working on their experiments in a tiny shed. She is determined to extract her precious uranium from the dull brown ore.

I hear Papa's slow footsteps on the stairs. "Are you ready, Juli?"

I had forgotten all about the dancing class. "No."

"Juli, please," he pleads from the hallway.

"I'm not going."

"Just try it once." Papa opens the door of my room. "Mama already paid for the lessons. Do you know how hard she tries to save money so that she can provide for you?"

"I never asked her to pay for dancing lessons."

Papa sighs. "Please, Juli, try to understand."

"Mama doesn't try, so why should I?"

Papa's eyes narrow. "She doesn't try? Juli, there you are wrong. Mama wants you to have all the chances that she never had. Is that too hard for a girl of twelve to understand?"

"But she doesn't try to understand what I want."

"And what is it that you want?"

For a minute I don't know what to say. "I want to discover things like Marie Curie," I mumble, showing Papa my book.

"And do you know why you have the time to read and write? That is because of your mother." Papa turns away from me. His voice is deep and quiet. "You are too young to understand all this, Juli. But you do understand how angry Mama will be at me if you don't go."

Mama will not talk to Papa or to me for several days. She'll mutter under her breath all day long. She'll yank my curly hair when she brushes it until my eyes sting. Papa will try so hard to please her, but the more he tries, the madder she'll get.

"I won't dance," I caution, "but I'll go."

Papa hugs me and spins me around. "Dance, not dance, what's the difference? The important thing is that you will go."

We take the number four streetcar to a neighborhood on top of the hill. The houses are big and far apart. We get off at the last stop, and Papa looks for the address. There is a small sign that reads *King Stephen Dance Studio*. Papa stops to catch his breath.

"What a beautiful spot," he says.

"If I didn't have to dance, it would be fine," I say.

"Try to enjoy it." Papa takes my hand. His eyes look far away as he scans the horizon. "When we were young, your mama and me, we had very little money. We wanted so badly to go dancing like all the other young people, but we couldn't afford the clothes, the shoes, the entrance fee. Only once, for Mama's birthday, we went."

"And did you dance?"

"Did we ever!" Papa's eyes are bright, and for a minute I can imagine him as a teenager with jet black hair and broad shoulders, and Mama the way I saw her in the picture on the dresser, with a flowing skirt and slender waist. "Remember, Juli, Mama always wants what's best for you."

Papa heads back down the hill. I could wait on this small bench until he comes back to get me. Who would ever know? I could walk down the street to the café and buy myself an ice cream cone with the change Papa gave me. His voice echoes in my head. *Mama always wants what's best for you.* From here on the hilltop, I can see most of Pest, the bend of the Danube, and the hills of Buda on the other side. I wonder about the village where Mama grew up. I don't even remember its name. She has never taken me there. Once I asked her, and she said we would have nothing to do there, no place to go.

Two girls open the door to the dance studio. I stand up, brush off the seat of my yellow dress, and go in.

There are mirrors along one wall. "All the girls over here, the boys over there," says the teacher in a loud voice. "Now let's pair off. Boys, go find a partner."

The boys hesitate. They don't know what to do.

"Is this too difficult? Walk across the room and pick the first girl you see."

A boy comes my way. I move back. He picks the girl next to me. There are more girls than boys, so the teacher tells the extra girls to stand on the side and watch.

The music starts, and the couples are moving all over the floor. Why are they taking dance lessons if they already know how to dance? *One two three, one two three.* The teacher asks one couple to go to the middle of the floor and show everyone how to do the foxtrot. *Up, back, flip, and turn.* The girl's dress sways with her hips. I wonder if Mama used to dance like that girl.

The teacher tells the boys to pick new partners and start over. I move back to the corner so again I am not picked. All the girls except me have on white shoes. I sit down at a small table and try to hide my feet.

Soon another girl with black shoes joins me. We watch the couples go by. "See that boy over there?" the girl whispers. "His face is as red as a tomato."

"More like a red pepper," I say.

"Or paprika," she says.

"Why aren't you dancing?" I ask her.

"I hate to dance. My mother made me come."

"Mine too."

The girl is named Mari, and she lives in one of the big houses around the corner. The whole time we are there, we never even try a dance step, but we have fun laughing at everyone else. The teacher glances over at us. We laugh quietly behind our hands.

Chapter Thirteen

When I get home, Mama is already back from Halas. "How was the dance class?" she asks.

"It was all right."

She takes my hands in hers. "Juli, Roza and her family were not there." Mama swallows. "The neighbor said that Roza's mother wasn't doing well. In fact, by the time the doctor got there, she was too weak to stand up. And her eyes were so sore that she could not open them."

"So where did they go?"

"Roza and her mother and her two brothers went to stay with their aunt in Lepence. Their father stayed back to take care of the farm."

I shut my eyes. The sound of the music at the dance class is still in my ears. *One two three, one two three.* Dancing couples swirl past. Even with my eyes shut I can see them and I can feel the light through my lids. Can Roza's mother see light? What about Roza? What if she goes blind too? How will they survive?

"We will find them in Lepence," I say firmly.

"I don't think so."

"Why not? We can take the train to Lepence and ask for the lace makers."

"And what good will it do us to find them?"

"We can give them money for a better doctor. We can bring them to Budapest to the eye clinic. There are lots of things we can do."

"Juli, the neighbor said that the aunt loves the children and will take good care of them and of her sister too. About the lace, she had no idea. We looked around the house, but all we found were a few empty bobbins."

"Is the lace all you care about? The dowry? The money you spent on it?"

"No, Juli—" Mama stops. She looks at me. Tears are running down her face, but she doesn't wipe them away.

"Juli." Papa's voice is louder than I've ever heard it. "Look at what you are doing to your mother. Look. Is this what you are trying to do? Hurt the mother who sacrifices everything she has for you? Answer me, Juli."

Papa takes my shoulders and shakes me back and forth.

Mama puts her hand on his. "Stop, Papa." She takes a deep breath. "Juli, listen to me. Now I will tell you something that maybe I should have told you a long time ago. You know I was born in the tiny village of Szendro. In my family we were three daughters—my oldest sister, Trudi, the second oldest, Erika, and then me. Trudi had a magnificent dowry, a whole trunk full of down comforters and embroidered linens. All the men for miles around were desperate to marry her. She picked a fine young man from Debrecen with blond hair and a big mustache." Mama sighs, remembering.

"Then came Erika," Mama continues. "She had a smaller dowry, two silver candlesticks, enough to find a handsome man from Miskolc. But for me, there was nothing."

Mama wipes her eyes. Her voice is low and quiet.

"My father decided that I would stay in Szendro and marry his friend, an old man with a big stomach and hairy ears. The poor man had lost his wife and needed somebody to care for his two sons. Father was having financial problems then. His pub by the railway station had very few customers, and his friend had money. I pleaded, I begged, I said I would work to earn my own money, but my father said no."

"What about your mother?"

"What could she say?"

"So how did you come to marry Papa?"

"I ran away. That's how." Mama is sobbing now. "I stole money my mother had saved for food to buy the train ticket to Budapest. I had a distant cousin…" Mama shakes her head. She cannot talk any longer.

Papa pulls her over to the sofa and she buries her face in the brocade pillow. Papa is rubbing her back. I want to know everything. I want to know whether her cousin let her stay. I want to know if she told her parents where she was. I want to know how she met Papa, a clerk for the city of Budapest. I want to know if she ever went back home. But Mama is done talking.

I sit quietly on the edge of the sofa, and a huge lump forms in my throat.

·

There is a squeaking sound coming from outside the door. We are quiet, listening. It comes again. Papa looks at me. We glance toward the door, and underneath it is a small white paw.

"The cat followed me home from the mailbox," I whisper.

"And you let him in?" Papa asks.

"I didn't let him in. He came in by himself."

"Must be a stray."

"I think he's one of Roza's kittens."

"Juli, that cannot be," Papa says. "A kitten cannot travel from Halas to Budapest by itself."

"I don't know. Maybe it's another cat that looks like him. But I think it's Bobbin, the kitten I liked so much."

Papa opens the door. Bobbin sniffs the air, walks elegantly over to me, and winds around my legs.

"You know how I feel about pets," Mama says, wiping her face with her handkerchief.

"You know, Mama, if this cat followed our Juli all the way from Halas, maybe he deserves our hospitality."

I can't believe Papa said that. He still has his arm around Mama's shoulder, rubbing gently, and she is leaning against his side.

"You know, sometimes I think a pet is very good for a child. She'll learn to think about something…outside of herself," Papa says, looking hard at me.

I have begged and pleaded so many times, but Mama always said no. I am waiting for her to pull her brows together and say to Papa, "What, do you want Juli to go around smelling like a zoo?" But this time Mama is silent.

I have thought so often about how happy I would be if only I could have a pet. But now the lump in my throat will not go away. Bobbin jumps up on the sofa and sniffs Mama. Then he steps gingerly onto her lap, turns around twice, and lies down.

Chapter Fourteen

What if Mama had married the fat man with the hairy ears? Then I wouldn't be me. I'd be half me, but that's not at all the same. And Mama would be different too. She'd be one of those ladies at the market that Sari was talking about, with a kerchief around her head and carrying baskets of peppers. Her skin would be brown and wrinkled from hoeing green beans in the hot sun.

I wonder if Mama cried when she ran away on the train to Budapest. I wonder if she left notes for her mother, for Trudi and Erika. I wonder what they are doing now. Is my grandmother still alive? And what about my aunts?

If I were to run away, I'd go to Halas and hide in Roza's barn. Whenever she came to work on her secret lace, she could bring me food. I'd play with the cats.

But if Bobbin is in Budapest, the rest of the kittens are probably gone too. And I couldn't just stay there without working on the farm. Roza's brother could barely carry the tools. I look at my thin arms. In gym, I can't do a single pushup. What would I do on the farm? Making lace doesn't require strength, but I don't think I could ever learn how to make the tiny stitches. Anyway, Roza is in Lepence. I wonder if she took her secret lace with her. Maybe it is still in the little bag behind the rafters in the barn.

With my quilt, I'm sweaty, but without it, I shiver. I take a sip of water from the glass beside my bed. When I set the glass down again on my nightstand, I see that there is a coin underneath it that is magnified by the water. The words on the coin are big and clear. Suddenly I know what Roza and her mother need—a magnifying glass so that they can see the tiny stitches without straining their eyes. But how can they sew and hold a magnifying glass at the same time?

The book about Marie Curie is next to my glass. I've already finished it, but I thumb through the pages. Marie was obsessed with understanding the nature of radiation. Even with two little children to take care of and a shabby laboratory, she persisted in her research.

I shut the book and stare at the coin through my glass of water. There has to be a way that the tiny stitches of the lace makers can be magnified and still leave their hands free. Of course, jewelers need their hands free too. When I was little, Sari and I used to play inside Lajos Bacsi's jewelry store. He had glasses with funny lenses that stuck out so he could see tiny diamonds. Once he let me try them on. I looked at my fingers and could see all the swirls of my skin. Those glasses—I see now that they are what Roza and her mother need. The special lenses jewelers use.

I put the book down and lie back on my pillow. Special

lenses would be very expensive. Roza and her mother could never afford something like that. I could ask Mama, but she has already spent so much money on the lace, and now who knows if it will ever be finished?

Bobbin comes softly into my room, jumps onto my bed, and curls up on my stomach. I pet his silky fur. How can I save money for the lenses?

In the morning, Mama doesn't ask me if I've slept well. She doesn't pour the milk for my cocoa.

"Did you sleep well?" I ask.

There are big bags under her eyes. "Not badly," she says, scrubbing the counter next to the stove.

"Maybe in a couple of weeks we can go to Halas and see if they are back."

"I think we should be done with that," Mama says. Her voice is tired and hoarse.

"Done with what?"

"The whole lace affair," Mama says. "You yourself said you don't want it. Papa says you are bigger now and we should let you decide things for yourself."

"But what about Roza's mother?"

Mama clears her throat. "Listen, Juli. I paid the lace makers well. With the money I gave them, they can pay the doctor."

"So I won't have a dowry?"

Mama is cutting onions for the soup. The knife makes a loud sound on the cutting board. "Drink your cocoa and get ready for school," Mama says.

I pour the milk into the cup. Some spills around the base, and I clean it up with a dishrag. I know I'm slouching over my cocoa the way I always do, but this time Mama doesn't say a word. Now she is slicing carrots. "Will you braid my hair?" I ask.

"I am tired this morning. Anyway, you are old enough to braid your own hair," Mama says.

I gulp the cocoa and stare into the empty cup. Now that Papa convinced Mama I am not a baby, she's given up on me. She doesn't care if I slouch or read without enough light or learn to dance. Maybe she thinks I'm doomed. No dowry, no husband, an old maid. My music teacher never got married. The girls call her an old maid and laugh at her rumpled skirts. I watch her hands move easily over the piano keys and wish I could make music like that.

I go to my room and brush my hair, but the part is crooked. I try again; it's no better. I can call Mama and ask her to help me, but she is busy making soup. Finally I braid my hair as it is. When I come out of my room, Mama doesn't even look up.

In the evening, Mama is scanning the *Budapest Gazette*.

"Looking for something?" Papa asks.

"I wonder if there might be a job for me."

"You already have a job," Papa says, patting her arm. "Right here, taking care of your husband and your daughter."

Mama points to an advertisement for a secretary. "Like maybe this one. I can type, you know."

"I know," Papa says.

"I didn't know that," I say.

"There is a lot about your mother that you don't know," Mama says. She turns to Papa. "Twelve years of a little here and a little there, all down the drain. Maybe I should earn it back."

"How do you know it's down the drain?" Papa asks. "I'm sure they'll finish the lace someday."

Mama turns back to the newspaper. I want to tell her that no matter what happens, the money has not been wasted. I want to thank her for saving the money and for helping me find the only friend I have ever had. But Mama does not look up, and I am quiet.

Chapter Fifteen

On my way home from school, I stop at Lajos Bacsi's jewelry store. "My dear Juli," Lajos Bacsi says when he sees me. "We've missed you. You know, your father doesn't win the chess games when you're not there to help him." He winks at me. "Too busy, are you, to spend some time on the corner with the chess players?"

Sari comes out from the back room. "What are you doing in Budapest on a school day?" I ask her.

"We have a special day off today, so Uncle Lajos asked me to help him in the shop."

"I see," I say, patting her arm in greeting.

"Hey, Juli, I want to show you something." Sari takes my hand and pulls me around the counter. "Look, I'm making a necklace." She lowers her voice. "It's for Mama, for her birthday." Sari has strung blue and pink glass beads. In the middle she is making a flower out of small white ones.

"It's very nice," I say.

Sari smiles. "I've missed you, Juli. Where have you been?"

"Nowhere, really."

"Your father said you are taking dancing lessons."

I don't say anything.

"Will you teach me how to dance?"

"I haven't learned yet."

Lajos Bacsi is helping a customer. One of the stones has fallen out of her bracelet. Lajos Bacsi puts on the funny glasses and looks at the bracelet under a strong lamp. He tells her to leave it with him and he'll have it ready in a week. When she leaves, I ask Lajos Bacsi how much his special glasses cost.

"These? I'd say around ten pengo or so. Why? Are you planning to become a jeweler?"

"I was just wondering. Where do you get such glasses?"

"The optician around the corner sells them."

Sari holds up her necklace. "It's done, Juli," she says.

I look up. In the mirror on the wall, I see Sari's little face with her front teeth missing and her brown hair parted perfectly on the side and her hand holding a sparkling necklace for her mother. Next to her is my broad face with frizzy hair all around and a crooked part down the middle. Suddenly I realize that Mama's birthday was last week, and neither Papa nor I remembered.

I take the long way home. The spring sun is warm on my back, so I take off my sweater and tie it around my waist. How can I ever come up with ten pengo?

"Hey, Juli."

I turn around. Coming up the hill behind me is Mari

from the dancing lesson. "Where were you last Saturday?" she asks.

"My mother forgot about the dance class."

"My mother didn't," Mari says. "But it wasn't that bad."

"Did you dance?"

She smiles. "With Paprika. And guess what? He's actually pretty nice." The blood rushes to her face. Then she shows me the package. "My mother sent me to buy a pair of white shoes." She takes the top off the box to show them to me. "The teacher said we're supposed to have them. So, will you come next Saturday? Please?"

"I don't know."

"Well, think about it." On a piece of paper she writes her address and tears it off for me. "Anyway, come and visit me at home sometime."

"Sure. I will."

As Mari heads up the hill, I call after her, "Hey, Mari—do you mind if I ask you, how much were those shoes?"

"These were on sale for eight pengo."

"Eight?"

"Yes. If you hurry and get them before the sale ends. I think they're usually nine or ten."

"Thanks a lot."

Before I get to my apartment building, I have a plan.

Chapter Sixteen

Mama is sitting at the kitchen table with the newspaper. She doesn't ask me why I am so late coming home from school, or how my school day was. I go into my room and find Bobbin asleep on my pillow. He stands up and stretches when he sees me. I pet him under his chin.

I sit at my desk and open my history book, but I can't concentrate on the Crusades. I have to ask Mama for the money for the dance shoes. I hate to ask her for something when she's already in such a bad mood, but it's not all my fault. I didn't cause Mama to be the third daughter with no dowry left. I didn't tell her to stay in Szendro and marry an old man with two sons. I didn't make Roza's mother get sick. I didn't ruin Mama's dowry plan.

I'll tell Mama that I cannot go to the dance class without the proper shoes. But what if she wants to go with me to buy them? Bobbin walks on the open pages of my book, sits down, and starts washing his face. He stares at me with his yellow eyes. I've never lied to Mama before. But really, it's not a lie.

The dance teacher did say that we should all have the proper attire. And Mama lied to her mother too, when she took the money for food and used it to buy a train ticket instead.

Outside my window the chestnut tree is starting to bud. Soon each little bud will have five or six leaves. The sun is stronger each day. Maybe Roza's mother is better now that spring is here. Maybe they don't even need the special glasses.

I go into the living room and sort through the mail. No letters for me. Mama is looking at the job notices in the newspaper again.

"Mama."

She doesn't look up.

"Mama, I need special white shoes for the dance class."

"I thought you weren't going."

"I'd like to try it again."

Mama looks up. "Is that so?"

"The teacher said we should have white shoes. They're on sale for eight pengo at the Crown Shoe Store."

"Eight pengo? My, they're expensive." Mama looks into my eyes. "And why have you decided that you want to dance after all?"

"I made a new friend there. Mari. She lives right near the dance studio."

"I see. So, that's the reason?" Mama sounds suspicious.

"Also, I think it's about time I learn, since I'm almost thirteen."

Mama smiles. "I think we can manage eight pengo."

Mama's old voice is back. She tells me to stand up straight.

She's worried about me again because of a simple lie.

"Juli, why don't you try some of that straightening oil on your hair?" she adds.

We go into the bathroom together. Mama helps me wet my hair in the sink and work the oil through. She massages my scalp with her strong hands, and then we comb my long hair over the bathtub.

"You know, Juli, you are a very pretty girl," Mama says, looking at my face in the mirror. "If only you would put just a little time into your appearance."

I look in the mirror. Mama's head is behind mine. We have the same crooked smile and oval face. Instead of frizzy braids, my hair falls in lush curls. Mama was right. The oil really makes a difference.

I cannot sleep. I never finished my history homework. What will I do in class tomorrow?

I can't believe how easily I lied to Mama. And she never said, "How about if I come with you to buy the shoes?" She never imagined that she had a daughter who did not tell the truth.

I sit at my desk and turn on the light. First I read the chapter of the history book and write a short summary. Then I take down the Arany Janos book and turn to the poem about King Matthias. When I read it, tears run down my cheeks. King Matthias' mother was so desperate to help her son. I wonder if he was as good as everyone says. I wonder if he ever lied to his mother.

I take out a clean sheet of white paper, and at the top I write:

Dear Mama,
Sorry this birthday present is so late. I think you'll like
this poem.
Love,
Juli

Then I copy all the verses in my best calligraphy. In the morning, when Mama gives me the money for the shoes, I will give her the poem.

Chapter Seventeen

When I wake up, Mama is already gone. She has left a note on the table: *Gone to my interview. Love, Mama.* I can't believe Mama is really looking for a job. I never thought she would go through with it.

The table is set with two mugs and two plates, for me and Papa. Next to my plate is an envelope, and inside are eight crisp bills. I go into my room and add two more pengo to the stack, the one from Lajos Bacsi and the one I found so long ago. Then I pick up the poem. I could leave it for Mama on the table. But suddenly I'm not sure. It will only remind her of the unfinished lace. I open the desk drawer and shove the poem inside. Then I put the envelope quickly into my satchel, gulp down my cocoa, and set out for school.

All day I can't concentrate on my work. In math, the teacher calls on me to put a simple problem on the board, and I don't even know which problem she's talking about. Although I read the history chapter, I can't remember in which year the crusaders were defeated. Kata and Agi look at each other. The teacher gives me a zero in her grade book.

At recess, I see Kata and Agi and Baba in their usual clump. For a while they ignored me, but now they are heading my way.

"We see your mind is on more important things, isn't it, Juli?" Kata says.

I pretend to read the history homework. Baba comes over and shuts the book. "We like the way you oiled your hair for him, Juli. Meet us after school so we can watch the first kiss."

Slowly they move away to the other side of the playground.

I try to be the first one out the door, but the teacher, Erzsi Neni, calls me back. "Juli, can I see you for a minute?"

My stomach flips. Everyone files out the door so I am the only one left.

"Juli, I notice that you seem preoccupied lately. Is there something I can help you with?"

"No, ma'am. I mean, no thank you. It's nothing."

She pats my shoulder. "Well, if there's something I can do, let me know. And Juli, here's a book you might enjoy." She hands me a fat volume called *Around the World in Eighty Days* by Jules Verne. "Have you read it?"

"No."

"Good. I wrote my address on the inside. When you're done with the book, come and return it and choose another book to borrow. We have quite a library, you know." She touches my shoulder again. "That's all."

"Thank you, Erzsi Neni. Thank you very much."

The title is in gold on a brown leather spine. I can't wait to go home and start the book. Maybe I should forget about the glasses. Maybe I should go to the shoe store and buy the white shoes like I promised Mama. Then I'll go to the dance class with Mari and forget about Roza altogether.

I feel for the envelope. It's still there. All I have to do is walk to the optician's office and take a look. I don't have to buy anything. Then I can tell Mama that the shoe store was out of white shoes and return the eight pengo to her.

Agi and Kata and Baba are there on the corner. I keep my eyes straight ahead and walk fast. "He's waiting for you, Juli," Baba says. Baba's younger brother is with them. "Ready for a kiss before the big day, Juli?"

I keep going. I walk faster and faster. They push the boy into me. "Kiss her, Miklos," Kata says. "Go ahead." But I am tall, much taller. My legs are long. I start to run.

"Go, giraffe!" shouts Kata. "Look at her go! Follow her, Miklos. Faster, faster!"

I can't stop, ever. I have to keep on running. But I'm almost out of breath. I hear footsteps behind me. He is close. I don't hear them laughing anymore. My heart is pounding and my legs are burning, but I won't stop.

Near the top of the hill I slow to a walk, but I won't look back. My legs are long; I can walk fast. The optician's store, the one with the big pair of glasses on the sign, is just ahead on the right. I plunge through the front door.

"May I help you?" asks a short lady.

I want to tell her everything. She is a complete stranger to me, but I want to tell her that three girls and a boy were chasing me and I barely got away. "No, ah, I mean, just a minute."

It's warm and bright in the office. The windows are so clean I can see every little leaf on the tree out front. The lady is cleaning lenses with a soft cloth and humming at the same time. It's a tune I know about a cow in the green fields. Her voice is thin and clear. She stops cleaning and looks at me. "Been running, have you?"

"Yes. I mean, do you have special glasses for jewelers?"

She looks at me strangely. "Did you say for jewelers?"

"Yes, please."

"For whom are you buying them, may I ask?"

I have to think fast. "For Lajos Bacsi, the jeweler."

The lady smiles. "Of course. You must be the niece I've heard so much about."

"No. Just a friend."

The lady takes several pairs of glasses out of the case. One pair is a little stronger, the other a bit weaker. I try them on. With the stronger pair, I can see every pore in my skin. Surely Roza and her mother will be able to see the tiny stitches.

"I think, ma'am, that I need, I mean, he needs the stronger pair."

Then I see that there is a small ticket with the price. Twelve pengo.

"I think I'll come back another day. He gave me only ten pengo today."

She waves her hand. "That is not a problem. I'll get the two pengo from him some other day."

She wraps the glasses carefully in paper and lays them gently in a box. I reach into my satchel and take out the envelope. I can say I changed my mind. I can leave and never come back. Inside the envelope are the bills. I count them slowly and put them on the counter.

"Please tell Lajos Bacsi that he can always return them if he would prefer a different pair," the lady says.

She has a kind face. I want to tell her about Roza and her eyes and lying to my mother. "Thank you," I say softly.

The lady hands the box to me. "Now, be careful on your way home."

"Yes, thank you. I will."

I put the box into my satchel and open the door.

Chapter Eighteen

By the time I get home, it is six o'clock and my feet are sore from so much running. I slip into my room and shut the door. I open my bottom dresser drawer and put the glasses in the back, underneath my stockings.

Mama is in the kitchen. "How was the interview?" I ask.

"I don't know, really. The lady said she would call me. Either she will or she won't."

"Oh, yes. The interview," Papa says. "I forgot."

"You forget many things," Mama says.

"Not the important ones," he says, kissing her hand.

Mama doesn't smile. "Can't you see that I am busy?" she says.

"Not too busy for a kiss," Papa says.

"Did you get the shoes?" Mama asks me.

"Yes."

"Did you make sure that they fit properly?"

"Yes."

"Good."

"What shoes?" asks Papa.

Mama smiles. "Juli has decided to go to the dance class after all."

Papa raises his eyebrows. "I see."

We sit down to supper. The potato soup is thick and creamy. The bread has a thick dark crust, just the way Papa likes it.

"Mama, you are the best cook in the world," Papa says.

I finish my soup quickly. "Juli, slow down," Mama says. "The food will not run away."

I put the spoon down slowly. "I wonder if after dance class tomorrow, we can go to Halas."

Mama stops eating. "Juli, we are done with the lace," Mama says softly.

I swallow the bread that has formed a ball in my mouth. "But I want to visit Roza and her mother. It has nothing to do with the lace."

Mama folds her napkin into smaller and smaller squares. "Juli, if we go, they will only feel bad. We paid them for a product that they did not deliver."

"Maybe they are still working on it."

"With the mother so sick she cannot walk? With eyes that are blind?"

"Roza is not weak or blind."

"Roza is a child like you."

"I want to go and see how they are doing," I say.

Mama is raising her voice. "You, who never wanted a dowry and never wanted to go in the first place? Now you want to go and make them feel like thieves?"

I want to tell Mama that I am the thief. I am the one who lies and steals, not Roza and her family. But my voice is completely choked up.

Abruptly, Mama stands up and gets her purse. "Here, Juli, is money for the train ticket."

"Maybe I should accompany her," Papa says.

"I don't think you want to miss a game of chess," Mama says.

The air in my room is still and humid. We have a fan in the storage closet, but I don't want to leave my room to get it. Bobbin sits on my windowsill and meows. I open the window to let him out, but he only sniffs at the air. "Bobbin Kitty, tomorrow maybe I'll see your mother and your brothers and sisters." Bobbin jumps off my bed and stands by the door.

I want to sleep, but each time I doze off, I think of Mama at the train station in Szendro, leaving her family behind. Then I think maybe it is me who is on the train.

When I finally wake up, it is past two in the morning. Bobbin is sniffing at my bottom drawer. I get up and put the box into my book bag. Tomorrow I'll go to the dance class and from there I'll take the streetcar to the train station.

Bobbin wants to leave my room again. I tiptoe over to the door and crack it open. What's that I hear? Are Mama and Papa still awake? After my eyes adjust to the dark, I see that they are sitting side by side on the sofa. Mama has been crying. Papa has his arm around her.

"She still needs us," Papa says softly.

Mama shakes her head.

"Believe me," Papa says. "A girl of only twelve needs her mother more than ever."

Mama is crying again.

"What is it?" Papa asks, rubbing her back.

"I think of how much I hurt my mother, my father, my sisters," Mama says.

"Shhh, Mama, that was a long time ago." Papa is rubbing her arm. "You know, Mama, times have changed. And we have to change with them or we will be left behind."

Mama wipes her eyes with the sleeve of her robe. Bobbin squeezes out the door and goes over to the sofa. He stands for a minute by Mama's feet and leaps daintily to her lap.

Papa smiles. "The cat found the best seat in the house," he says.

Bobbin looks right at me with his big yellow eyes. What is he trying to tell me? Should I go out to the living room and tell Mama and Papa about the glasses? Should I return them to the optician? How stupid to have wasted Mama's money on special glasses for someone I may never see again in my life. Should I even go to Halas tomorrow?

I lie back down in my bed, turn on the light, and start *Around the World in Eighty Days*. In the first chapter Phileas Fogg simply tells his friend, "We are going around the world." Someday I will take a long trip. I'll go in an airplane and land somewhere far away. Australia, Africa, America—who knows?

When I wake up in the morning, my light is still on. The book is open on my stomach, and Bobbin is sleeping on top of the book.

Chapter Nineteen

Mari is happy to see me at the dance class. "Did you get the shoes?" she asks.

"Not yet."

"That's all right. I bet she won't even notice."

As soon as the music starts, Paprika comes over and asks Mari to dance. Her feet fly over the linoleum. How did she learn so quickly? She is laughing and having fun. When the music stops, they come over to me. Paprika introduces me to his friend Janos. "May I have the next dance?" he asks me.

The blood rushes to my face. "I—I—no, thank you."

"Are you sure?"

"Yes."

He shrugs and asks someone else. I slip out the door into the afternoon sun. I'll just take the streetcar to the train station. The dance teacher will never notice.

The train to Halas is more crowded than usual. On the seat next to me is a lady with three very skinny sons. One is sleeping, and the other two are fighting with each other. The lady slaps their hands. Ordinary people, the kind Mama doesn't like. Across from me is an elderly gentleman dressed in old trousers with suspenders. He tips his hat to me, and for a minute, I feel grown up.

Outside the fields are turning yellow. Ladies with babushkas on their heads are working in their gardens. A little boy waves at the train and I wave back. I see three ladies with their heads covered pushing bicycles stacked with lettuce. For a minute, I imagine Mama like them, with layers of skirts and brightly colored scarves. If Mama had stayed in Szendro, she would be one of those ladies. And I would be one of those little children walking in the muddy street.

I should have brought a sandwich. My stomach is growling. I open *Around the World in Eighty Days*. Mr. Fogg and his friend are in India. They buy an elephant and ride off into the forest. My stomach feels queasy from reading, so I look out the window. Here the farms are smaller, shabbier. They are clustered together into a sort of village. I wonder if this is the kind of village Mama grew up in.

How could Mama have saved enough money for my dowry, dance lessons, white shoes? She should have spent that money on something for herself. A new pair of shoes. A shiny skillet. I sit up straight in my seat. If Mama were here, she would say, *Juli, stop slouching.* Suddenly I wish she were. I would say, *Mama, tell me about your sisters. What were they like? Your father? Your mother?* I would ask her if we could visit them someday.

I am worried about my trip to Halas. What if Roza isn't

there? What if she and her family never came back to the farm? And if they are there, what will I say? That I've come to say hello and deliver some funny-looking glasses? What if they don't accept my gift? It seems like years ago that Roza refused the poem I wanted to give her. What if, as Mama says, they feel bad about taking our money?

The station at Halas looks shabbier than I remembered. I feel confused. Which way is Roza's farm? I look up the main road. To the left, wasn't it? Everything looks different as I head away from the station. What if I get lost? I could wander in the countryside for weeks without ever finding my way.

Up the road I see their barn, so I run, but the satchel is hurting my back. The lenses—I almost forgot. They could break if I fall. I walk more slowly up to the front door of the house and knock. Nobody answers. I go over to the barn. The mother cat is asleep on a bale of hay. Another fluffy white cat is chasing a bug on the barn floor. That must be the one Roza liked so much.

A boy comes into the barn. I think he is from the neighboring farm. "They're gone," he says.

"Do you know when they'll be back?"

"The father comes back at night."

"Can you give him a letter for his daughter?"

"What letter?"

"Just a minute." I look behind the milk pail. There is no bag. I look behind the blanket, and there is Roza's pencil hanging by a piece of string, and the notebook that I gave her with the story in it. I tear out a piece of paper and smooth it with my palm. Then I write in clear printed letters:

> *Dear Roza,*
> *I came to see you, but you're not back yet. Bobbin is with me in Budapest. Mama says not to worry about the lace. I hope your mother is better.*
> *Your friend,*
> *Juli*

I hand the letter to the boy. He puts it into his pocket. "Their mother went blind, you know," he says.

"I know."

He shrugs.

It takes forever for the train to come. Two men are smoking on the platform. One of them winks at me. I look around. There's nobody else there. Why did I ever come to this deserted town?

Chapter Twenty

When I get back to the station in Budapest, it is dark. I had better hurry home or Mama will worry.

When I open the door of our apartment, Mama is washing the dishes and Papa is reading the newspaper. Nobody asks me about the dance class, the train ride, my visit to Halas. I fix a salami sandwich and eat it standing in the kitchen. Mama doesn't tell me to eat more slowly, to chew each bite, to sit down and take my time.

I go into my room and put the special glasses into the drawer. Maybe Monday I will try to take them back. Then I'll get the white shoes in time for next Saturday's dance class.

The telephone rings. It is probably Papa's sister, my aunt Erzsi. She calls almost every Saturday evening. Suddenly I am so tired that I don't even feel like reading. I lie down on my bed, turn my head to the wall, and sleep.

"Juli, I want to see the white shoes."

I must be dreaming.

"Juli." It's Papa's voice. "Where are the shoes?"

I open my eyes. It's dark in the room.

"Where are the white dance shoes you bought last week?"

"They must be in the closet," I mumble.

Mama turns on the light and starts throwing my shoes into the middle of the room. Sandals, boots, school shoes. That's all. She comes over to the bed and pulls me up by the arm. "Now you will find the dance shoes."

"I must have lost them."

"How can you lose shoes that were on your feet?"

"The dance teacher called," Papa says, "to offer us a pair of white dance shoes. She thought that perhaps we couldn't afford them."

My stomach drops. "I never bought them," I whisper.

Mama is shouting that she raised a thief. She is shuffling through all my dresses, throwing them off the hangers.

"Where, then, is the money?" Papa asks calmly.

"I bought glasses."

"Glasses? Eyeglasses?"

"For Roza's mother," I whisper.

Mama stops. "The lace again," she says, leaving my room. She slams the door behind her.

I open the door and shout after her, "I'm not a thief!"

"What do you call somebody who lies and steals?" Mama shouts.

"She's only a girl who was trying to help her friend," Papa says.

"And hurt her mother."

I hear the front door of the apartment open and shut, and then the door of our building. Papa is in my room again, standing under the light, his arms hanging limply at his sides. I want to say something, but I cannot stop crying.

When I wake up, it is already after ten o'clock. I am afraid to go out of my room. I read until I am so hungry that my stomach hurts. When I go into the kitchen, there is a note on the table. *Papa is playing chess. I am at work. Mama.* Not *Love, Mama.* Not *Here is a slice of fresh bread for your breakfast.*

I cut myself a thick slice of bread and spread it with butter and jam. I can hardly believe that Mama has a job. She has always been home when I am there, cooking, mending, cleaning. Now our apartment is empty. Except for Bobbin, that is. Come to think of it, where is he? I go outside and call him, but Bobbin is not at home either.

I sit at my desk and do my homework. Math problems, history summaries, and finally the one I like best, Hungarian. We are supposed to write an essay about an event that changed our lives. I list all the possibilities:

When Papa's father died.
When I fell down the basement steps and broke my arm.
When I learned to read.

None of them seems very interesting. Maybe the reading one, but I can't really remember before I could read. Mama always says I was born reading.

Bobbin is meowing at the window. I open it wide and feel the moist air. It might rain soon. Bobbin steps onto my blank paper. At the top I write:

When I got a cat.

It sounds like a babyish topic, I know. I've read about children who beg their parents for a pet, and finally for their birthday they get a tiny puppy or a fuzzy kitten. I stroke Bobbin. This cat is different. This cat found me. This cat is a messenger from my friend.

I start to write about the lace dowry, how Mama insisted on it although I didn't want it at all, how I dragged my feet on that first trip to Halas but then met Roza there. I write about Mama being from the country and almost having to marry an old man because she didn't have a dowry. Suddenly I know that I need to know more. What was Mama's life like in the small village? Why doesn't she ever go back? How did she meet Papa? How did she learn to be a secretary? I cannot finish my essay if I don't know.

When Mama comes home, she prepares onion soup without saying a word.

"How is your new job?" I ask.

"Fine."

I ask Papa about his chess game. "Did you win today?"

"Not today. Not since you stopped helping me." He tries to joke, but I can hardly smile.

We eat in silence. Then I go back into my room and reread the essay. There are too many holes. I go back out to the kitchen. Mama is wiping the stove.

"Mama?"

She looks up.

"What was it like in Szendro?"

She shrugs. "A city girl like you doesn't care."

I look at Mama. "Please, can you tell me?"

Mama keeps scrubbing at a stain. "It was a long time ago, Juli."

"Not that long," I say. "How did you meet Papa?"

Finally Mama talks, but without looking at me. She tells me how her cousin said she could stay with him for one month, so she went to a class to learn how to type. She practiced there every day for hours until she could type faster than everyone else in the class. The city of Budapest needed a secretary to help the clerk in city hall, and they selected the best student in the class.

Papa interrupts. "And that was your mother."

At midnight, we are still talking. It is past two in the morning when I finish my essay. I put it into my notebook for Monday.

Chapter Twenty-One

I try to forget about Roza and her family. Maybe the boy never gave Roza my letter. Maybe he used the paper to wrap his salami.

My third-quarter report card is all "1"s except for a "3" in domestic skills. I am especially bad at embroidery and handiwork. The thread tangles, and the fabric gets dirty from my hands. I wonder how Roza ever made those beautiful white stitches.

When I get home from school, nobody is there. Mama doesn't get out of work until after five. At first I like coming home to the empty apartment. I fix myself toast with jam and read the newspaper. No one pokes my back and asks me to sit up straight. No more questions about the boys. But after a week I miss hearing Mama's voice greeting me even before I've had a chance to step past the threshold.

On Sunday, Mama and Papa go to visit my aunt Zsofi, but I stay home to study. We have a big exam on Monday in world history. I make study guides and reread almost two hundred pages in the textbook.

My eyes are tired. I rub them and try to go on to the next chapter, but the words are blurry on the page. I stand up and look into the mirror. My hair is a mess, and my eyes are red like Roza's. I go into the bathroom and splash cold water on my face. Then my cheeks are blotchy. Of course no boys look at me. Why couldn't I have gotten soft hair like Mama? Then there's my height to consider. I tower over all the boys. Mama says they'll catch up to me someday, but when?

I put the history book aside and pick up *Around the World.* I only have two pages left, and I've been saving them. I hate to finish a good book because then I can't read it anymore, but I can't stop my eyes from following the words on the page. Mr. Fogg is almost home. He has saved a woman, and she has become his wife. At the very end the narrator asks if the journey was worth it. He says, "Truly, would you not for less than that make the tour around the world?"

I close the cover and feel the smooth leather. Maybe someday I can collect books. I'll have a small shelf by my bed of all my favorites so I can reread them anytime I want.

I stand and stretch. It's seven o'clock but still light. Inside the book is the address of my teacher. She said I could come and pick out another book. She said she had a whole library. I leave a note on the kitchen table so that Mama and Papa will know where I am, and I head out the door.

The breeze is warm. I breathe deeply and smell the lilac bush on the corner. Mama always says lilac is a smell from heaven. I get onto the streetcar at the bottom of the hill and take a seat. A man and his daughter are in the seat ahead of me. The girl reminds me of Sari with her missing teeth. I haven't seen her in a long time. Maybe I'll go visit the jewelry shop next week.

Simon Street. I get off and look around. There are lots of old buildings close to each together. I've never been in this neighborhood before. I check the address. Number fifty. I follow the street almost to the end, and there it is, an old apartment building set back from the others. I ring the doorbell.

"Juli, hello. I'm so happy to see you. How did you like the book?"

"I loved it."

Erzsi Neni leads me into her apartment. It is two rooms, and from floor to ceiling the walls are covered with books. She introduces me to her husband, who is reading at the desk. "My husband teaches at the university," she says.

"Erzsi has told me so much about you," he says. "She says you are one of the smartest students she's ever had."

I blush. "Thank you, Professor."

"Coffee, tea, or milk?" Erzsi Neni asks.

"Anything is fine."

"Let's go for the coffee then," she says, pouring three small cups. She sets a bar of chocolate on the table. The professor opens it, breaks it into pieces, and offers me one. Then he asks me about the Jules Verne book and other books that I have read. He knows all about Admiral Byrd and Marie Curie. He pulls a book off the shelf.

"How about this one?"

It is a thin blue volume called *Joan of Arc*.

"Do you know about her?"

"A little."

He hands me the book. "Take it. See what you think."

"Thank you, sir."

"Not 'sir.' Call me Istvan Bacsi."

"Thank you, Istvan Bacsi." I stand up. "And thank you for the coffee, Erzsi Neni. Now I think I had better go home or my parents will worry."

My teacher and her husband walk me to the front door of the building. "Come again, Juli, anytime."

"Thank you. I will."

It is almost dark when I get home. Mama and Papa are sitting on the sofa.

"Did you get a new book?" Papa asks.

"Yes. About Joan of Arc."

"She was a very courageous woman," he says.

"What are you reading?" I ask, noticing that Mama is holding a small book open on her lap.

"It's from Aunt Zsofi," Mama says. "A book of quotations."
I sit down next to her on the sofa.

"I like this one," Papa says. "*Take advantage of the day at hand because it won't be back tomorrow.*"

"That's you," Mama says.

"Well, it's true, isn't it?" Papa asks.

"To a point," Mama says. She turns the page.

Papa reads the next one. "*All's well that ends well.*"

"I like that one," I say. It feels nice to be sitting next to my mother. Bobbin jumps up onto the sofa. He sniffs at Papa and then at me, and finally he curls up on Mama's lap.

"Worse than a baby," Mama says, petting him under his chin. We listen to him purr.

"I didn't know you liked cats," I tell Mama.

"When I was a little girl, we had a cat that I liked quite well," Mama says.

"What was her name?"

"We called her Tiger."

"Was she fierce?"

"She pretended to be," Mama says. Then she tells me about how her sisters used to see who the cat liked best. They'd sit around her and entice her with bits of yarn.

"And who did she choose?"

"Usually me," Mama says.

"Just like Bobbin," I say.

Chapter Twenty-Two

Mama tries to convince me to go with her and Papa to my uncle Zoli's for the day, but I have too much homework.

"Juli, you study too much," Mama says, touching my cheek. "You have dark circles under your eyes. Take a break."

"I can't."

"Papa, tell her."

"She won't listen," Papa says. "Just like her mother."

"I'd say she inherited that trait from both of us," Mama says. "Juli, at least turn on the light when you read. And sit up. You're all hunched over those books." Mama turns to leave, but then she calls back from the hallway, "And heat up the soup for lunch. Don't forget."

"I won't."

After Mama and Papa shut the door, the apartment feels too quiet. I try to concentrate on the words in my history book, but Bobbin keeps getting in my way.

"Bobbin, we already went through this, remember? You have to let me study."

Bobbin meows at the door. I open it, and he sits down as usual. I sigh and pick up *Joan of Arc*. It is 1431, and Joan is only a little older than me, but she is not afraid to dress up like a boy and stand up for what she thinks is right.

The door of the building opens. Maybe Mama and Papa forgot something. But the footsteps are too light. "Is this apartment three?" a voice asks.

"Upstairs," says the janitor.

Then I see her blond hair so wispy and bright in the sunlight coming through the window, and her thin green dress, and Bobbin purring and rubbing on her legs and mine, around and around.

At first we don't know what to say. I offer Roza some lemonade, but she says she is not thirsty. I ask her to sit down, but she refuses. Remembering how she refused the poem about King Matthias, I blush. I wish we were in the barn sitting together on a bale of hay. Finally Bobbin jumps onto the table and meows. "He's telling you to sit down," I say.

Roza sits on the edge of the sofa, and I sit next to her. "How's your mother?" I ask.

"Better." Her face lights up. "The doctor gave her a special salve for her eyes, and we moved back home."

"I went to see you a couple of weeks ago," I say, "but you weren't there."

Roza nods. "I know. I got your letters. With my brother's help, I read all of them. I know about Bobbin and everything." She looks down. "Sorry I never answered. You know, my writing. I never had a chance to practice."

I don't say anything. Roza knows I could have read through her misspellings.

"No, truthfully, it's not that," she says. "Mama told me it would be best not to answer, in case, in case…we never finished." Roza looks up into my face. "But guess what, Juli?"

"What?"

Roza takes a brown parcel out of her net bag. Then slowly she takes the knot out of the string and unrolls the paper. There's a layer of thin white paper under the brown. I start to see the raven's wings, completely open, soaring, with the ring in its mouth. Around the raven are cherry trees and daffodils and lilies of the valley.

"Roza, it's so perfect."

Roza shakes her head. "Not perfect at all. Some of my stitches got too loose and others a bit too tight. But, overall, we are pleased."

"How did you ever finish with your mother's eyes so bad?"

"She did a little in the morning. I worked all afternoon. My aunt helped in the evening. And then at the end I added a surprise."

I touch the thin lace with my fingertips. There are woven stitches and chain stitches and tiny dots. The branches of the cherry trees are wound around each other. The lily flowers fall like small bells. The daffodils are open on their stems. "I have no idea."

Bobbin jumps onto the table and starts to put his paw onto the lace. "Not for you, Kitty," I say sternly, pushing him back with my elbow.

"He's showing you something," Roza says.

My eyes follow his paw. Next to the last cherry tree in the corner of the square is a lace kitten. "I can't believe it," I shout, the blood rushing to my face. "You put your secret lace into my dowry!"

"I didn't even tell Mama." Roza looks away. We don't know what to say. "Juli, can I ask you something? What are you going to do with our lace if you don't get married?"

I look out the window. There's a maple tree with tiny buds and behind it another apartment building like ours, and beyond that is the Danube, and beyond that the fields and farms and the whole rest of the world. "Maybe I'll get married or maybe I won't. I don't know. But wherever I go, I'll take your lace with me."

"I thought so, but I just wanted to be sure."

"Hey, I have a secret for you too, Roza." I lead her into my bedroom and open the bottom dresser drawer. Behind all the stockings is the box.

"Open it. Go ahead."

Roza takes the top off the box and removes the tissue paper.

"Put them on. Go ahead," I say.

"For me?" Roza looks unsure.

I pick up the glasses and put them onto her face. Roza squints for a minute. Bobbin stands in front of her and meows.

"I can see the designs in his eyes," she says. "Like lace threads around the pupil."

"They're for you and your mother, so you can see the stitches."

"But these must be very expensive."

I put them back into their box. "Hurry. Put the box into your bag. It's a secret." I shove the box into the bottom of her bag.

"Are you sure…" Suddenly Roza jumps up. "Oh no, Mama told me to take the six o'clock train back to Halas."

"But wait. We have to pay you for the lace."

"You paid us so much already. You know, your mother sent us all the money for the lace in the mail plus extra too. And then we were so late with the dowry…" Roza is standing near the door. "I'd better go."

Bobbin rubs against Roza's legs. I don't want her to leave so soon. "How do you think Bobbin Kitty got to Budapest?" I ask.

"I don't know. Papa said he took the kittens to a farm down the road, except for the white one."

"I guess Bobbin preferred an apartment in Budapest."

"He was looking for you. Remember how in the barn he always went right to your lap?"

"I remember."

Roza leans forward to hug me with her skinny arms. "I'd better go or Mama will be worried."

Then, taking a last look at the lace on the table, Roza heads down the stairs.

"Thanks for the glasses," she shouts. "Thanks a lot."

"Bye, Roza," I shout down the dark stairwell.

I watch her out the window until her green dress is just a tiny speck. Then I sit with the lace on my lap touching the stitches, tracing the thicker thread around the raven's massive wings. How did they do it? Even with two good eyes, it seems impossible. The raven is flying over everything, the cherry trees, the flowers, the cities and farms, carrying the precious ring.

Will Roza come back and visit? If I write, she might not answer. She never has time to practice her spelling. Maybe I'll take the train to Halas again someday. Maybe by then the mother cat will have had another litter of kittens.

Bobbin is asleep on my open history book. I pet his head between his ears and wait for Mama and Papa to come home. I'll show them the lace. I'll tell them that Roza's mother is better. I touch the tiny stitches. So many hours and hours of work.

I take down the Arany Janos book and open to the first page. *You will go far.* But right now I don't really want to go anywhere. I want Mama to come home so we can look at the lace together. I want to read her the Arany Janos poem. Then Mama will fix supper and I'll do my homework. Mama will say, *Juli, sit up straight. You're slouching.* I pet Bobbin and wait for my mother to come home.

Author's Note

When I was a child, my grandmother told me she had something very special to show me. In the bottom drawer of her dresser, wrapped in brown paper, was an exquisite lace tablecloth. This is the story she told me.

When her daughter, my aunt, was a child, my grandfather worked for a short while in a small town in Hungary called Kiskunhalas, or Halas, for short. This town was well known all over Europe for its lace making. My grandparents were not wealthy. In fact, money was always a problem. However, my grandmother decided that she would commission a lace tablecloth for her daughter as part of her dowry. This way when it came time for my aunt to get married, she would own something of value and thereby become a more desirable choice for a wife. The lace makers in Halas refused at first, saying that they could make only small lace doilies, but my grandmother insisted. Finally, through her persistence and the offer of a steady income, the women agreed.

This lace tablecloth is now framed on the wall in my aunt's house. She took it to a museum curator in New York who said that it is one of the biggest and most exquisite examples of Halas lace ever made.

When I went to Hungary in 2004, I visited the lace museum in Halas, and truly there were no pieces anywhere close to the size of my aunt's tablecloth. The women there told me about the history of lace making in Halas.

Lace making has a long-standing tradition in Hungary, but the specific technique of sewn lace making was developed in Halas in the late nineteenth century. Instead of using bobbins to form the patterns, a teacher at the Halas grammar school, Arpad Dekani, borrowed the Italian method of sewn lace making and combined it with traditional Hungarian motifs.

First a pattern is drawn with ink onto onion-skin paper. This paper is stitched to linen and stretched over a needlework frame. Then special linen thread is used to form the contour of the design. When the skeleton of the design is done, the linen is taken off the frame and the paper is removed. Using very fine linen thread that is made especially for the lace makers of Halas, various stitches are used to fill in the spaces between the contours.

The peasant women in Halas learned the lace-making techniques from their mothers and grandmothers. The work was very hard on their eyes, and many of them showed the strain of hours of tedious work each day. Today, a group of women including two mother-daughter teams make lace in the museum workshop for eight hours a day. They told me that it is very hard on their eyes and the pay is low, but there is very little other work to be had in Halas, so they continue the tradition of their ancestors.

The Lace Dowry, although fiction, is based in part on the story of my aunt's lace.